RAIDERS OF BLUE DOME

OTHER FIVE STAR WESTERN TITLES BY ROBERT J. HORTON:

RAIDERS OF BLUE DOME

A WESTERN STORY

ROBERT J. HORTON 1881-1934

FIVE STAR
A part of Gale, Cengage Learning

GALE
CENGAGE Learning®

Detroit • New York • San Francisco • New Haven, Conn • Waterville, Maine • London

GALE
CENGAGE Learning·

LIBRARY OF CONGRESS CATALOGING-IN-PUBLICATION DATA

Horton, Robert J., 1881–1934.
   Raiders of Blue Dome : a Western story / Robert J. Horton. —
First edition.
    pages cm
    ISBN 978-1-4328-2632-1 (hardcover) — ISBN 1-4328-2632-8
(hardcover)
   I. Title.
PS3515.O745R34 2013
813'.52—dc23
                                2012050956

Published in conjunction with Golden West Literary Agency.
Find us on Facebook– https://www.facebook.com/FiveStarCengage
Visit our website– http://www.gale.cengage.com/fivestar/
Contact Five Star™ Publishing at FiveStar@cengage.com

Printed in the United States of America
3 4 5 6 7 17 16 15 14 13

ADDITIONAL COPYRIGHT INFORMATION

★ ★ ★ ★ ★

Part One

★ ★ ★ ★ ★

CHAPTER ONE

For an old cow town, Ransford looked the part. Its main street dozed in the warm, spring sunshine, dusty and deserted. The cottonwoods along the thin, muddy stream that flowed along its southern boundary rustled their leaves languidly in the breath of wind that idled across the wide prairie from the western hills. To eastward the rounded outlines of Blue Dome Butte showed grayish-green against the grass, already turning brown. The sky was flawless, the color of light blue glass, with the sun a dazzling disc of gold. Some cattle, a little distance on the level plain to northward, furnished the only sign of life.

It was the dead hour of noon. The false fronts of the few buildings—hotel, general store, café, bank, resorts—on the short main street stared at each other across a thoroughfare empty of human beings. Even the dogs, usually plentiful, had scattered to the houses behind the business structures. The hitching rails were bare. A few horses munched their hay in a corral behind the livery barn. That was the one indication that there was anything unusual to be associated with the town of Ransford this day. For it was not the custom to put horses such as these in the corral. The fact that they were there showed that the barn was full, and the fact that the barn was full was evidence there were many people in town. They were big, powerful horses, the kind of mounts favored by stockmen.

Another indication that something extraordinary was afoot could be seen in the appearance of the Rodeo resort. The Rodeo was the great meeting place in Ransford—the chief rendezvous for weary and thirsty cowpunchers and all others who came to the town. There were other resorts, to be sure, but the Rodeo was the largest. It had the longest bar with the largest mirror behind it; it had the most gaming tables and the greatest variety of games; it had a lunch counter so that its patrons might not have to leave it when hungry. And this day its swinging doors were backed by a solid wooden barrier, and it was locked. The other resorts were open as usual.

Behind its locked door the Rodeo presented a most unusual appearance. The gaming tables had been piled, one upon the other with their tops meeting, in the two rear corners. This left a large space between the bar and the wall of the room, and the space was filled with chairs. Every chair was occupied by a substantial citizen of the Blue Dome country. There was a table in the front of the room, and two men sat there, one directly behind it and the other a little to his left. They faced the other men in the chairs.

At the moment there was a complete silence, save for a soft swishing sound made by a ruddy-faced man in a white apron, who was wiping the bar with a damp towel, while watching the others covertly. Gray hairs were plentiful below the wide hat brims of the men in the chairs. Some frowned, and others stared at the man behind the table, obviously the chairman, with an open-mouthed air of expectancy. All were serious, the man behind the table, red-faced from exposure to wind and weather, large of build, gray eyes, clean-shaven, with a firm chin, the most serious of all. This man now cleared his throat and fingered the soft brim of his hat lying on the table.

"We'd better understand just where we are," he said slowly. "As president of the Teton Stockmen's Association I want everything made clear to those members who live on the outskirts of our range and who have not been molested. I don't know when we have had such a big turnout at a meeting, and I don't know if there ever was a special meeting of the association called before."

He looked at the sea of faces before him inquiringly, as if he expected to hear a supporting voice.

"We can thank Bolt Blodgett for *this* one," somebody said, grinning.

"Go ahead, Cameron, put it up to the sheriff," called another.

The man at the president's left shifted uneasily in his chair and settled his hat more firmly on his knees.

"I'm listening, Cameron," the sheriff said to the man behind the table.

"Very well," said Cameron, "we might as well put it square to you, Sheriff." He rose from his chair, eyed the slender, blue-eyed man with the long, sandy mustaches, on his left, for a moment and again turned to the rows of faces before him.

"Gentlemen, we all know that we've been fighting the Blodgett gang for three years. Blodgett has stolen our cattle right and left, drove 'em across the line into Canada, and laughed at us. He's took what horses he wanted. He's shot every man on the Blue Dome range that had the nerve to try to beat him to the draw. He's outrode or out-maneuvered every bunch we stockmen have sent after him and every posse Sheriff Strang here has put on his trail. One time he loses himself in the badlands off in the southeast. Next time he lights out for Canada, and again he slopes for the mountains, after scattering his gang of cut-throats to the four winds. But he always comes back. Those of you who range a long ways in the east and south, and who haven't been bothered so far, can expect to be visited by Blodgett almost any time."

There was a murmur of confirmation from the men in the chairs. The sheriff sat, looking straight ahead, with a frown on his face. Once he opened his mouth as if to speak, but desisted.

"To get right down to cases, gentlemen," Cameron continued, "this Blodgett has us whipped to a standstill at present. We can call on the state authorities, and we can call on the state association, but I reckon we don't want to do that. We've always been pretty independent up here. It's all right for us to know we're whipped, but that's no sign we want the rest of the world to know."

Voices greeted this with approval. Sheriff Strang's frown deepened.

"There's just this much to it," said Cameron, clearing his throat impressively. "The thing has come to a showdown. Now there are two ways out. One way is to get to Blodgett somehow and ask him what his price is to get clean out and away. . . ."

"Not as long as I've got a head of stock or an acre of range!" shouted a man in the rear of the room. The sally brought a cheer.

Cameron nodded his head. "I thought you boys would feel that way about it. That's the way I feel myself. If we bought him off, I don't reckon I'd want to be president of the Teton Stockmen's Association again. The other way is to fight him!" He brought his fist down on the table as the men, with the exception of the sheriff, cheered lustily.

"And there's only one way to fight him!" shouted Cameron. "There's only one way to fight him, now that the law is licked!"

Sheriff Strang leaped to his feet as the cheering died suddenly. "What can I do?" he cried. "I've hunted Blodgett high and low! I've sworn in extra deputies till I've had to order a barrel of new badges. I've tried tricks. I've planted cattle, as you know, and while we were laying for Blodgett and his gang, they've run off with half a beef herd somewheres else. I've worked night and day to corner him, but he's always got the tip. The range is honeycombed with spies." He paused as he saw scowls of disapproval on many faces. "If it ain't that, it's that

Blodgett is uncanny when it comes to getting the scent of a posse," he amended, dropping into his chair.

Cameron nodded to him. "That's it, Sheriff," he affirmed. "We ain't blaming *you* none. You've done your best, just like the rest of us. But that doesn't help. We're up against it. At first it was individual ranches, now it's wholesale rustling and killing, and it's a matter for the association as a whole. Blue Dome range is being ripped wide open by a gunfighting cut-throat who don't care a rap for sheriffs or any other kind of county or state authorities. If we take our men off the spring roundup to try and corral Blodgett, he'll sneak away to one of his hiding places for a time until things quiet down and be at us again. We can't stop work at this season. It all comes right down to this. Bolt Blodgett is the brains of the outlaw outfit. If we get Blodgett, we'll break up the gang. The thing is to get Blodgett!"

"That's what I've been trying to do," the sheriff complained.

"And that's what *we've* been trying to do," said Cameron, with a wave of the hand that included all the others present. "But I think we've been too conspicuous at it. Our moves have been an open book to everybody on Blue Dome range. Maybe we'd be better off if we went after him in his own style . . . with a gun and one man."

The sheriff looked up quickly, and the men in the chairs leaned forward with interest.

"One man . . . the right man . . . could do for Bolt Blodgett," said Cameron slowly, scanning the faces.

Everywhere he saw nods and looks of approval. "He's got every man on the range spotted," scoffed the sheriff.

"I know that," said Cameron in a cold voice. "To send one of your men, or one of *our* men, would be murder."

"You . . . you propose to *import* a man?" the sheriff asked. "A gunman?"

"I propose that the association import . . . employ . . . a

special agent," Cameron replied amid a deep silence.

"Same thing!" exclaimed the sheriff. "I wouldn't stand for it! That's just as bad as calling in the state to help us out. What would they think of me outside the county? I can't be a party to any such step."

"You wouldn't have to be," said Cameron coolly. "This is a meeting of the Teton association at which you have reported that you can't get Blodgett or break up his gang. The association has the right to act as it sees fit for the benefit and protection of its members."

"You mustn't do it!" cried the sheriff, rising and slamming on his hat. "I won't have any imported gunmen . . . any professional killers . . . in my territory. Oh, I know what you're thinking!" He scowled into the sea of faces. "You're thinking that you elected me, and that it's up to me to keep my mouth shut an' one eye closed. I won't do it! What'd they say about it outside? Wouldn't they say I was a fine sheriff? Wouldn't they . . . ?" and his voice trailed off into an inarticulate growl.

"As I said, Strang, we're not blaming you a bit," Cameron soothed. "So far's I'm concerned, I'd vote for you again. There's no politics in this. This thing would be too much for any sheriff. And who's going to tell 'em outside? You bet we're not going to spread the news. Other local associations have done what I suggest. Goodness knows, the state association has enough on its hands. . . ."

"I didn't say I couldn't break up the gang!" the sheriff flared. "I haven't broken it up yet, that's all. But I haven't quit."

"Meanwhile, we're losing stock," Cameron pointed out dryly. "We've just come through a hard winter. We had to borrow strong from the bank . . . all of us. We're in pretty deep, and we can't afford to lose stock. Every beef counts like sixty now. This Blodgett is a plain outlaw. There's a price on his head. He's dangerous . . . a menace. He killed two of my men . . . two of my best men. I don't feel that I want to lose any more men, and I reckon the others feel the same way. I can't see any way out of it except to hire a man who will give him a run for his money at his own game."

"I won't have it!" declared the sheriff, striding past the rows of upturned faces as the man in the white apron hurried to the rear door to let him out. He stopped near the door and spoke in a loud, angry voice. "If you bring in a gunman, I'll lock him up first chance I get! I'll take after him, that's what I'll do. I won't have it, that's all. And I'm going to keep after Blodgett!"

He stamped out the door that the bartender shut after him and locked. Cameron looked at the other members of the association with a quizzical expression.

"It's the only remedy I know of . . . now," he said quietly in a very sober voice. "It's a sort of last resource, I reckon, but . . . what do you gentlemen think?"

An uneasy silence followed the putting of the question. Then: "Who would we get?" asked a gruff voice in the assembly.

Cameron moved his hat, fidgeted with his watch chain, puckered his brows, and leaned on the table with both hands, staring at them keenly.

"I'd suggest . . . Lennister!" he said suddenly in a ringing voice.

As though the sound of the spoken name were a signal, every man present started and drew a deep breath.

"Lennister?"

The name was whispered back and forth, uttered in low, awed tones, mouthed and mumbled while men looked searchingly into each other's eyes and back to the stern face of the man leaning on the table. The man behind the long bar dropped his towel and stared furtively at the reflections of the association members in the big mirror.

Then came a loud laugh that sounded forced, and a harsh

voice: "Can you see Strang jailing Lennister?

"Let the word get to Blodgett an' he'll probably light out of his own accord," chuckled another.

"We ain't got enough money to hire him . . . in cash," said someone.

"The bank'll stake us to protect itself," came from the rear.

Will Cameron pounded on the table for order and suggested a ten-minute recess to think it over and partake of refreshment. The motion carried with a whoop.

CHAPTER TWO

The rapid and thorough dissemination of news and rumors in the wide spaces of the West is a thing at which to marvel. Without the aid of telephone or telegraph wires, or even mails, reports of happenings and news of individuals will spread with extraordinary rapidity through a section where one can travel miles and leagues on end without so much as a sight of a human being. It is a mysterious mouth-to-mouth means of communication, part of which is innuendo, with opinions veiled and suggested rather than openly expressed.

Thus had the reports and rumors concerning Lennister permeated every space and corner of the far-flung Blue Dome range. They were conflicting in some ways, these reports. None in that district had seen Lennister in the flesh. He was variously spoken of as being tall or short, with the preference favoring the report that he was tall; he was said to have black, flashing eyes that one could not forget once he had looked into them; but then, again, it was contended that he was a blond; he was somewhere between twenty-five and thirty-five, it was thought, yet there were those who insisted he must be all of forty, if not more. He rode a magnificent iron-gray horse, a sorrel, a pinto, a satiny black, or a bay, according to who it was that was describing him; he was a two-gun man, he was a one-gun man in the same way.

But all reports agreed in one respect—Lennister was a gunman without a peer from the Mexican border to the Canadian line. Talk had it that no eye was quick enough to follow the movements of his draw; that for him to miss a mark, no matter how difficult or small, was an absolute impossibility. He was also gifted as a trailer, and was without fear.

Lennister—no one had ever heard a first name applied to him—was supposed to have drifted north from Texas or New Mexico. There were wild rumors concerning his past: a fugitive from the Texas Rangers, a former cardsharp, an outlaw, a train robber, a reformed bandit who had turned professional gunfighter because of the desire for excitement. Anyway, he was credited with the breaking up of rustling bands in Wyoming, with the killing of outlaw leaders in southern Montana, and was said to have succeeded remarkably well as special agent for the cattlemen's organization in the Musselshell country, south of the Missouri. Last reports had it that he was headed north, and that his gun was for hire.

Cameron's announcement was not entirely unsuspected in some quarters, for several of the cattlemen had discussed the matter before the meeting this day and had agreed that Lennister was the man to send for and to put on the trail of the formidable and elusive Bolt Blodgett.

"Might as well get the best . . . or the worst . . . whichever way you want to look at it," Sam Butler, owner of the Three Bar, had told Cameron on the latter's Triangle A Ranch on the way to the meeting in town.

Cameron, who had lost heavily in stock, and who had buried two men shot to death by the outlaw, had been desperate. Twice he had sent every man he had after Blodgett and his band, and had gone himself.

The sheriff had had to move but a finger and the Triangle A outfit was at his disposal. It all had availed nothing.

During the recess Cameron made himself plain to other members of the association. Were they to be driven out of the stock business by Blodgett and his gang? Were they to submit to the infamy and ignominy of buying him off? And, if they *did* buy him off, would his word be good? Other stockmen backed Cameron in his contentions, and, when the meeting reassembled, it seemed a foregone conclusion that a motion to send for Lennister would be unanimously passed.

There was a hush of expectancy as Cameron pounded the table with his fist for order. "Mister Butler, of the Three Bar, wishes to make a motion," he announced, nodding to the ranch owner, who stood up and glared about fiercely beneath bushy brows.

"I move that it's the sense of this meeting that what's done here today we keep to ourselves," said Butler loudly, with a heavy scowl at the man behind the bar, who moved hastily into the little front office.

The motion was carried immediately after being seconded.

"It seems to be generally agreed that we send for Lennister," said Cameron. "Now if there are any questions before we put it to a vote, sling 'em so we can have it over with."

"How we going to find him?" piped a voice.

"The larger ranches will send two men each to towns south of the river to look for him," replied Cameron. "Some of the men are pretty sure to get wind of him. He'll be brought to the Triangle . . . my ranch . . . and the proposition put up to him."

"How much will we have to pay him?" asked one of the stockmen.

"There's two-thousand-dollar reward offered for Blodgett now by the county and three thousand more offered by the association. That's enough in itself to make him sit up and take notice. He may have heard of it already and be considering it. If necessary, we'll offer five thousand more and apportion it according to the number of head of stock each member has. We can club the bank into taking care of that part of it . . . the cash, I mean."

"What about the sheriff?" came the question.

"The sheriff isn't a member of the association," said Cameron dryly. "But we're hoping Strang won't object to a little of the right kind of assistance."

A tall, thin man with drooping mustaches and languid blue eyes rose from his chair in the rear of the room and fixed Cameron with a fishy stare.

"Us fellers who are away off in the east end of the range . . . ," he said in a plaintive tone, and then looked about at the faces turned toward him in surprise, "we ain't been bothered yet, an' we ain't none too well off, bein' in the drought belt. I don't reckon I'd be able to pay much to bring in this here gunfighter, an' I wouldn't want him visitin' my place, for one, an' maybe drawin' Blodgett down on me." He looked about again uncertainly, opened his mouth as if to say more, closed it, and sat down suddenly.

Cameron frowned, and his frown was reflected in the faces of others. "I explained how the extra expense would be met . . . if we have to sweeten the reward money," explained Cameron. "We don't want to work a hardship on anybody, and those who've been hard hit by the drought needn't chip in at all. There's some money left in the association treasury, too." He was trying to place the man who had complained, and finally remembered him as being a rancher by the name of Rounce, who had a place southeast of Blue Dome Butte, at the edge of the badlands.

"Fair enough," said Sam Butler in a loud voice. But Rounce had gotten to his feet again. "How do we know that this feller Lennister wouldn't make a dicker with Blodgett an' double-cross us?"

It was a question straight to the point, one that had occurred to others there, although none had expressed it in so many words.

Rounce sat down, tugging at the ragged ends of his mustache nervously.

Cameron was visibly annoyed. "It's a chance we're taking," he quickly snapped. "Lennister didn't double-cross the Musselshell outfit so far as I can learn. It doesn't stand to reason that Blodgett would offer to buy him off when he thinks that there's no man living that can beat him to the draw. He's pretty near right in that respect too. But Lennister has a reputation, and if Bolt Blodgett is as vicious as he makes out to be, he'd be looking for a chance to take a crack at Lennister. Gunmen are jealous *hombres.* That's in our favor."

He wiped his face and brow with a bandanna handkerchief after this lengthy speech and scowled at his audience.

Sam Butler rose. "I move that we send for Lennister and leave the fixing to Cameron," he said in his harsh voice.

"Second the motion," cried a score of members.

Cameron took a vote by members, and every one of them voted for the motion with a single exception. That exception was Rounce.

"No!" he shrilled when his name was called from the roll.

Cameron hesitated with a slight flicker of his eyelids before he continued reading from the roll.

"The motion is carried!" he announced as he finished. In that moment he felt his first tremor of doubt.

A minute later the meeting adjourned.

As Cameron rode toward his ranch in the gathering dusk, after the sunset, he found himself beset with misgivings. The contrary vote of Rounce bothered him. What was the matter with the man? Was he fearful of an expense that he would incur? Or was he so afraid of Bolt Blodgett? Why, the man had no spine. The chief of the rustlers had doubtless cut through Rounce's range more than once on his way into the badlands. Of course, he hadn't bothered him. The man had no cattle worth bothering with to speak of. Yet his had been the one vote cast against the motion to import Lennister.

Cameron was aware of another disturbing thought. He had been a leading spirit—*the* leading spirit—in the proposal to bring Lennister to Blue Dome. Wouldn't that be sufficient to inspire the wrath of Blodgett if he should hear of it? Wouldn't it be sufficient to bring Blodgett and his band of desperadoes down upon the Triangle at the first opportune moment? Cameron was not so foolish as to underrate the outlaw's ability, or his capacity for hate. He knew Blodgett would stop at nothing to satisfy his own personal aims. The outlaw leader was ruthless, vengeful, daring, and unafraid. He had painted his own reputation with black deeds and foul killings until it was a stark, sinister, menacing reality—a thing to be feared and reckoned with.

In the deepening twilight Cameron rode between herds of his breeding cattle on the Triangle range. The cattle had been moved in for the branding. It was not safe to leave unbranded calves too far from the main ranch, lest they be driven away and the mothers killed or taken along on the Outlaw Trail across the Canadian line in the north. The Triangle was a continual delight to Cameron's eye, for he had made it in the long years after the terrible winter of 1885-6. It was the finest ranch, and the best stocked, on the whole Blue Dome range.

The first stars were gleaming in the purple curtain of the night sky when he rode down the road from the bench to the fertile bottom north of the stream where the ranch house and other buildings were located in the shelter of the bluffs. Tall cottonwoods grew along the stream and about the rambling ranch house. The scent of the growing grain in the fields was sweetened by the faint perfume of flowers as he neared the front of the house.

He breathed deeply and dismounted slowly, somewhat stiff from his ride. For Will Cameron was no longer young.

A man came in the direction of the barn in the rear to take his horse. As he mounted the steps to the verandah, a girl came running out the door. She threw her arms about his neck and kissed him on the cheek.

"I was just going to send some of the men to look for you, Daddy," she said in a musical voice. "What made you so long, Pops?"

"Business," said Cameron in a gentle voice. The stern lines in his face softened as he looked at her radiant beauty in the light that filtered through the screen door. He stroked her hair for a few moments. Then, as she pouted playfully and seemed about to ask more questions, he said: "Go inside, Connie sweet, and tell the cook I'm as hungry as a coyote in winter."

"I've looked after your supper myself, Daddy," she said gaily. "And I've made you a surprise pudding."

"I'll be right in," he promised.

For some moments after his daughter had gone into the house to arrange his supper, Cameron stood on the porch, looking above the weaving tops of the cottonwoods at the star-splashed sky. His eyes were troubled and his lips pressed tightly. But he threw back his shoulders and walked with a firm tread as he entered the house and took his place at the head of the table.

CHAPTER THREE

In the morning Cameron was up at dawn, giving his orders to his foreman. Later he would look in on the branding himself, but first he wanted time to make his plans for the sending of the messengers who were to look for Lennister or get word to him. He decided on two trusted and tried men of his outfit and told the foreman to leave them at the ranch to await his orders.

Soon after breakfast two men rode in from Sam Butler's ranch. They said Butler had told them to wait on Cameron's instructions. Cameron told them to put their horses in a corral until he was ready for them and went into the house.

He felt nettled at Butler. Why hadn't the Three Bar owner ridden down to help him plan the disposition of the messengers? It would have been no more than right. He remembered that it was Butler who had made the motion that they send for Lennister and leave the details to him. Well, after all, he was president of the Teton Cattlemen's Association, and it was probably his duty. But confound Butler, and confound Rounce!

In his little office in the front part of the house Cameron studied the state map, and particularly the vast domain south of the Missouri, and north of the Missouri to the Teton, the river that ran south of the Triangle. Somehow he could not shake off the feeling that Lennister had crossed the Missouri and was in one of the small towns in the strip between the two rivers. He jotted down the names of some towns on a memorandum sheet and took care that the messengers, or scouts, would cover the

24

territory for the whole distance from the mountains to beyond the badlands in the east.

Other men arrived from other ranches, and Cameron took them all into the bunkhouse and explained where they were to go and what they were to do. He assigned different men to the several towns, with instructions to return when thoroughly satisfied that Lennister was not in the town they visited—providing they could get no word of him. They were to follow up any clue to his whereabouts. But they were to exercise caution, and under no circumstances were they to deliver their message to anyone save Lennister himself. This was extremely important, Cameron pointed out, thinking at the same time that he would be glad to be rid of the business. If Lennister was found, he was to be escorted to the Triangle.

Cameron felt another twinge of misgiving as he watched them ride away on their mission. It was a more dangerous business than he had reckoned, this importing of a gunman. Suppose he should find himself unable to control Lennister? What kind of a man must he be? A professional killer. He would have to be careful when he was on the ranch to keep him away from his men—from his house. He almost wished that the messengers would be unsuccessful. But the thought of Blodgett's depredations, his sneering disregard of life, his scornful confidence and audacity brought the grim lines back to his face and the hard look into his eyes. All was fair in fighting a man of that stamp!

Before noon all the messengers had been dispatched. Cameron rode out to where the branding was in progress, looked on for a time silently, and then rode back to the house. His mind was not on the ranch work. His thoughts were somewhat confused and apprehensive as he anticipated the arrival of Lennister. Connie Cameron noticed this and tried to worm out of her father what was on his mind.

But she was the last person on earth he would think of telling what was in prospect. He was resolved, too, that Lennister would not meet the girl. She would not even see him if he could help it, but he doubted his ability to conceal the presence of a stranger at the ranch. Since the death of his wife he had permitted Connie to have pretty much her own way. She knew as much about the ranch business as he did. The mere mention of Bolt Blodgett's name was enough to make her eyes flash fire and bring the hot flush of anger to her cheeks.

The balance of the day and the next passed quietly enough. But at sundown next day three riders galloped up to the ranch from the trees along the stream and brought up in the courtyard.

Cameron came out of the house hurriedly and immediately saw that it was his own two men who had returned first. With them was a stranger, and he felt a thrill of excitement as he looked at this third man. He was tall, gray-eyed, dark-haired, with clean-cut features and a clear, bronzed skin. His hat, soft shirt, riding boots, and chaps were of undeniably good quality. But the holster on his right was old and worn, though still durable, and the butt of his gun hung free at a rakish angle.

As he completed his swift inspection, Cameron saw one of his two messengers shaking his head meaningfully. "No luck, boss," he said. "Couldn't find a trace of our man, an' so we beat it back, accordin' to orders. This party was in town an' said he was lookin' for a job, so we brought him along. Seems like a good sort," he added in an undertone.

Cameron, to his surprise, felt relieved. They hadn't found Lennister nor got word of him then. The man before him looked capable. He could use a capable hand. But none of this showed in his face, which was sternly inquiring.

"You've worked cows?" he asked, motioning to the other two to take away the horses, and noting, too, that the newcomer's mount was a splendid bay gelding with life and fire and breeding.

"Too many of 'em," came the drawling reply that hinted of southern ranges.

"Where from?" asked Cameron, suspecting that he had detected a note of flippancy in the other's reply.

"South," was the short rejoinder.

"That covers a heap of territory," Cameron remarked with a trace of sarcasm.

"I've done the same," said the stranger cheerfully. "I don't stay put long. I'm not looking for a foreman's job . . . yet."

An air of independence that bordered closely on the insolent radiated from the man. But his teeth flashed in a good-natured smile as he spoke. Cameron was impressed by something he couldn't define, but which, he concluded, was the suggestion of ability. The man looked able enough and young enough. A keen look from the gray eyes told Cameron that here was no ordinary line rider. He could certainly use a good man, regardless of where he came from, if he would stay until the beef shipment in the fall.

"What's your name?" he asked curiously.

"Trenton," was the immediate response without hesitation.

"Sounds like a city I've heard of somewhere, but. . . ."

"New Jersey," the other put in quickly. "Born there and named after the burg, I guess. You want a pedigree?"

"I want a certain amount of respect from the men who work for me," said Cameron gruffly. "Put your slicker pack in the bunkhouse. I'll take you on. My foreman will see you later. You can eat with those two you came with."

He turned abruptly and started for the house. When he looked back over his shoulder, he saw Trenton standing, holding a partly rolled cigarette in motionless fingers, staring at the front of the house. Cameron looked and caught sight of a white dress on the porch and a last golden gleam of the sunset lighting his daughter's face. He stopped and looked behind angrily.

But the new hand was strolling toward the bunkhouse, whistling. When Cameron resumed his walk to the house, Connie had vanished.

Before dusk two other messengers had returned and announced their ride as fruitless. Cameron felt a certain elation and, at the same time, a peculiar sense of disappointment. It occurred to him that if the quest for Lennister proved futile it would make rather a fool of him. He had started something and the association would look to him to finish it. He had the reputation of being a finisher. The Cameron breed was firmly rooted among the West's pioneers.

Such were Will Cameron's thoughts as he sat in his little office as the twilight deepened into night and the stars came out above the cottonwoods. He thought, too, how sweet the air was, how peaceful the ranch with its sounds of late chores being done, and the soft breeze sighing in the leafy branches of the trees.

Then the peace of the ranch was rudely shattered by the pound of hoofs, and a film of dust came in the window from the courtyard.

Cameron could see no sense in such an obstreperous arrival, and he was in an irritable mood as he went out on the porch to see who had come to the ranch in such a fashion. A harsh voice met his ears.

"Mind! See that that horse gets the best! Understand?"

It was an unfamiliar voice that jarred on the ear. It was ominously pregnant with a tone of command. Cameron felt his anger rising. Who was it that thought he was privileged to talk like that on the Triangle?

"Where's the old man?" demanded the aggressive voice.

Cameron stepped down from the porch as three men approached him. Before they reached him, however, he had remembered, and the feeling of misgiving seemed to swell in his throat.

He recognized two of his messengers following a stranger who was in the lead. One of the messengers nodded his head in excited fashion and pointed to the man ahead. On the instant Cameron became cool and collected. He even felt antagonistic.

"What is it?" he asked sharply, staring at the stranger.

They came to a halt, and Cameron saw a pair of small, beady eyes, jet black and flickering, regarding him coldly. They were set rather close together above a long, hooked nose that resembled the beak of some predatory bird. The face was lean and dark, clean-shaven, with lines from the nostrils down to either side of the cruel mouth with its thin lips and drooping corners. The man was tall, somewhat stooping, as if weighted down by the two heavy guns strapped to his thighs.

"You Cameron?" came the question, almost insulting in its very sudden brusqueness.

"I'm Cameron," replied the stockman tartly. "And you, I suppose, are . . . Lennister?"

"Forget it," snapped the other in a tone as penetrating as the thrust of a rapier. "Don't speak that name again." His hands had dropped like a flash of light to the butts of his guns. He whirled on the two messengers. "Get out of this," he commanded.

Without giving the men a chance to obey, he drew back suddenly and his right fist shot out, catching one of the men on the jaw and knocking him backward so that he stumbled to his knees. The man's eyes flamed red, and he remembered just in time. His hand hung above his gun as he got to his feet and backed away with his companion.

"Look after your horses, boys, and get something to eat!" Cameron called above his visitor's jarring, jeering laugh of scorn.

"I don't call that a good introduction to a man of your reputation, Lennister," said Cameron coldly. "If you're going to start in that fashion, I don't reckon we'd better do any business."

The two-gun man peered at him in sneering contempt. "You think I'd ride half a day for nothing, Cameron? You sent for me. I'm here. You better think twice about whether we can do any business or not." There was an ominous ring in his voice—a threat.

Cameron thought swiftly. Well, what could he expect? Wasn't the man a professional gunman, and a two-gun man at that? A wave of disgust went over him. Then he thought of Bolt Blodgett. Here was evidently a man of Blodgett's caliber, only worse. Wasn't that what the association wanted? Hadn't that been a part of the plan—to get such a man as this?

Cameron looked behind him at the house. The front was still dark.

"Come into my office," he said in a more amiable tone. Then he led the way to the verandah.

At the supper table, in the bunkhouse, Trenton was listening with mild interest to the excited recital of the two men who had brought Lennister to the Triangle.

CHAPTER FOUR

Cameron closed the door and pulled down the window shade in the little darkened office before he lit the lamp. He stepped back from the table, sat down at his desk, and motioned his obnoxious guest to a chair.

"How am I to know for sure that you are Lennister?" he asked in guarded tones as the man sat down and looked curiously about the office.

"Your men took pains enough to find me," was the reply. "I didn't know you wanted to see me until they ferreted me out. I might not have come if they hadn't mentioned this association of yours up here. I don't work for nothing, Cameron." He scowled darkly, and his gaze reverted to the small safe that stood between the desk and the window in a corner.

"We don't expect you to work for nothing," said Cameron, studying the gunman. "There's a . . . a hard job up here." He hesitated. But didn't he have the backing of every stockman on the range, with the possible exception of Rounce? "Still, it hadn't ought to be such a hard job for you," he added with an attempt to smile.

The man's features were repulsive, his look snaky, and the grin that trembled on his thin, bloodless lips was evil. The backs of his thin hands were hairy and the fingers seemed never still. He possessed all the appearance and the attributes of the professional killer. This was what Cameron thought, and he repressed a shudder with difficulty. It was his first experience with a man of this sort.

"What do you want done?" asked the other pointedly.

"Well, Lennister. . . ."

"I told you to can that name," his visitor broke in. "There's no need for advertising. Get me? Everything's got ears. Now get down to business. Call me anything . . . Smith, that's good enough. Just call me Smith."

"Maybe you're right . . . Smith," said Cameron. "I suppose it would be a dead give-away if it got around that you. . . ."

"An' tell that pair of clods who brought me here to keep their mouths shut," Smith interrupted in a growling voice.

"Of course," Cameron agreed. "I'll give 'em their orders. I understand, then, that your guns are . . . for hire?"

"What do you want?" asked Smith impatiently. Cameron frowned, then he leaned toward the other and spoke distinctly in a low voice. "There's an outlaw tearing this range to pieces by the name of Bolt Blodgett. Ever hear of him?"

Smith, as he called himself, stared darkly for a few moments and then nodded.

"All right," said Cameron, somewhat relieved. "Blodgett's a wild number. He's a first-class cattle thief, a bandit, and a killer. He's the fastest man with his gun that was ever heard of in these parts, unless it might be yourself. That's why we decided to send for you."

"You want me to kill Blodgett?" Smith asked bluntly.

Cameron moved uneasily in his chair and avoided the man's glittering eyes.

"That it?" Smith prompted. "You want Blodgett bored?"

"We . . . want him out of here . . . want him stopped." Cameron's voice gained strength. "We've got to fight him at his own game," he said in a hoarse whisper. "He's killed every man that's tried to draw with him. We sent for you to find him, drive him out, or. . . ."

"Kill him," sneered Smith. "You don't need to come right

out and say it if you're scared to. What's in it for me?"

"The county offers two thousand dollars reward, and the association offers three thousand on top of that," said Cameron. "That's five thousand." Somehow or other it didn't seem such a large sum of money as Cameron mentioned it.

Smith's short laugh was mirthless. "All of that?" he jeered. "How long would it take this Blodgett to get away with five thousand dollars' worth of cattle on this range, eh? How much has he cost you so far, eh? Is the association broke?"

Cameron's face darkened with swift anger. "You know better than that," he said sharply, forgetting to keep his voice lowered. "And you ought to know that this is the season when we're short of ready cash. We can't pay no big fortune for this job. How much do you want?"

Smith's eyes gleamed shrewdly. "That's talking, Cameron. I know all about this ready cash business. But I know your outfit and the county can raise ten thousand, too. That's the price."

Cameron smiled wryly. It was an odious business at best. There seemed nothing else to do but to agree to the gunman's terms. There had seemed nothing else to do but send for him when Cameron had advocated the move at the association meeting. The situation had not changed since. Yet Cameron resented the cold, dictatorial attitude of the man. Were it not for the others in the association, Cameron felt he would rid himself of the whole business. And buy Blodgett off? Never!

"All right," he said with a frown. "Ten thousand it is. I reckon it'll be worth that much to get rid of Blodgett. But remember one thing, Len- . . . Smith, I mean . . . we would rather *capture* Blodgett and jail him. We want you to try to capture him."

"Sure," said Smith sarcastically, "I'll try to capture him. How's this money to be paid?"

"In cash, when Blodgett is delivered," replied Cameron with a look of surprise.

"Where you going to pay it?" Smith demanded.

"Why . . . at the bank in Ransford, of course. That's where our business is transacted."

Smith shook his head. "Won't do," he said gruffly. "I want my money as soon as I deliver Blodgett . . . day or night, understand? Any hour of the day or night. I don't hang around a place long after I've finished my work. And I don't go prancing in no towns to banks and such public places in a case like this. You get the money here. Put it in that safe you've got there. Tend to it tomorrow or next day, for I'll be going out. I don't lose no time. Where does this Blodgett hang out?"

"If we knew that, we wouldn't be dealing with you," said Cameron. "Sometimes he's in the badlands southeast of here, sometimes he's across the line up north, and now and then he's in the mountains off west. He'll be hanging around, though, now that we're not out looking for him, and with a mess of unbranded calves all over the range. If he doesn't get wise to you, you ought to be able . . . say, Smith, I understood you were a pretty good trailer."

"You've told me enough," growled Smith. "Tell your men to keep hands off and their traps closed. I'll run this thing. All you got to do is tend to the money end of it. I want something to eat and a bed." He rose and stood with the yellow gleams of the lamp casting a lurid glow on his dark, repulsive features. His hooked nose more than ever resembled a beak. His hands fell lightly to the butts of his guns.

"I'll have the cook fix something for you in the bunkhouse," said Cameron, rising. "And I'll get you a bunk out there. But I want you to leave the men alone, Len- . . . Smith, I mean. I want that understood."

"What's the matter with my staying in the house?" Smith asked insolently.

"The house is for my family," said Cameron with a flare of

temper. "That's to be understood, also."

"Oh, all right," sneered Smith. "I'm all right to do the dirty work, but I'm not good company."

"You will be well paid," said Cameron, struggling to keep control of himself. He blew out the light in the lamp and led the way with stealthy step out of the office into the hall and through the door to the verandah. Then they proceeded to the dining room of the bunkhouse.

As they entered the bunkhouse, the new hand, Trenton, strolled around the front of the house and stood for a few moments in the starlight under the waving branches of a cottonwood. He saw a white vision framed in the front doorway. It was Connie Cameron, staring at his tall, graceful figure with a worried look in her eyes. He caught a glimpse of her eyes in the starlight, and she, in turn, got a good view of his profile as he touched a match to his cigarette. He strolled toward the porch, but the white vision disappeared. He went on to the bunkhouse.

Sometime afterward Cameron entered with the gunman. Most of the men in the room were asleep in their bunks, but the light still burned in a bracket on the wall. Trenton and another were the only ones up.

"This is Mister Smith," said Cameron shortly. Then to his scowling companion: "There are several vacant bunks. I'll see you in the morning."

Smith glowered at Trenton and the other man, then looked about the place.

"I'll take this bunk by the door," he announced brusquely.

Cameron turned to go, but stopped as he heard Trenton's voice.

"That bunk is taken," Trenton drawled, rocking on his high heels.

Smith whirled on him with a snarl. "I just said it was," he snapped, thrusting out his jaw.

The amiable light in Trenton's gray eyes hardened and shaded to green. He pointed to the bunk. "That's my slicker pack there," he said slowly, without his drawl. "A man's pack is enough to hold his bunk, I reckon."

"Is it?" sneered Smith. He leaned over, jerked the small pack from the bunk, and flung it on the floor.

Trenton's move was so swift that Cameron did not suspect his intention until he saw Trenton land squarely on the point of the gunman's chin. He cried out to Trenton as Smith's hands dropped like lightning to his guns.

The light flickered for an instant on hard metal in Trenton's hand and then went out to the accompaniment of a crash of shattered glass a moment before Smith's guns roared in the darkened room.

"Stop it!" shouted Cameron. "Trenton, get out . . . you hear me? Get out! Don't shoot, Smith. Don't . . . !" He paused, and the room echoed with the startled exclamations of the roused cowpunchers. "Silence!" roared Cameron. Then, as the sounds died away, he struck a match. A breath of air from behind him put out the flame. He struck another and held it high. He saw the gunman crouching at the door leading into the dining room, with both his weapons held at his hips.

Trenton was sitting calmly on the disputed bunk, with his slicker pack by his side. The long, blue barrel of the gun held in his right hand rested on his left forearm. He looked steadily at Smith.

"You might have hit one of these other fellows," he drawled.

The match went out in Cameron's hand, and he heard Trenton move instantly. But there were no blinding flashes from Smith's guns, as he had expected. The cook came in from the dining room carrying a lighted lamp.

Cameron was suddenly angry at Trenton. One or more men might have been killed or wounded because of his crossing the gunman. The stockman motioned to Smith to put up his weapons and glared at Trenton, who quickly returned his gun to its holster.

"Move out of that," he ordered peremptorily. "Take another bunk." He flashed a warning look at Smith as the other men in the room stared hard at the newcomer.

Trenton made no move. He stood beside the bunk, looking at Smith from between narrowed lids. Then, as Cameron was about to shout at him in a rage, he laughed. He picked up his pack and tossed it into a vacant bunk on the side of the room. The cowpunchers looked at him with widened eyes, half admiringly, half curiously.

"Orders are orders, I reckon," drawled Trenton, "when they come from the right quarter."

Cameron shook his head in warning at Smith. The signal was not lost on the men. Then, as Smith moved to his bunk with an evil grin on his thin lips, Cameron appeared to hesitate, as if he did not know what to do or say next. Finally he went out, swearing softly to himself under his breath.

CHAPTER FIVE

In the cool night wind Cameron felt more at loss than ever. He asked himself if Lennister—or Smith, as he wanted himself called—was the kind of man he had expected to see. He decided that he was. A professional gunman—a killer—could hardly be expected to be anything else than brutal, overbearing, self-contained, and egotistic. He would naturally want men to fear him, to cringe before him, since it was the only glory he could command. And yet there was something about Lennister, or Smith, that was not satisfactory, not wholly convincing. And the man, personally, was repugnant and repelling.

There was the matter of the cash money, too. Lennister, or Smith, had been adamant in his demand that it be brought to the ranch and held in readiness for him at a moment's notice. Well, Cameron, and the other members of the association for that matter, would be glad to get rid of him as soon as possible after Blodgett had been delivered. Cameron shrugged uneasily as he remembered the look in the gunman's eyes when he had mentioned the delivery of the outlaw. He had no intention of delivering him alive.

Trenton, too, was a source of worry. He had spunk, that fellow, Cameron thought. He hadn't had any tea-party look in his eyes when he had spoken to the gunman about the bunk. That had been a quick draw and a sure shot when he had put out the light with a bullet before his antagonist could get into action. It had been a clean blow, too. Cameron did not doubt but that

Lennister, or Smith, had Trenton marked. He hadn't let Trenton off just because Cameron had demanded it. There would be trouble in that quarter.

As Cameron mounted the steps to the verandah and passed into the hall, Trenton came out of the bunkhouse and disappeared under the cottonwoods.

Cameron had no sooner lit the lamp in his little office than he was startled by the appearance of his daughter in the open doorway. He avoided her eyes with a feeling of guilt as he saw the accusing look in them

"Daddy, who is that man?" she asked, entering the office and confronting her father at close range.

"What man?" countered Cameron, trying to think of a way to avoid telling her what he suspected she already knew.

"That man who was in here," she said seriously. "You forgot to talk low, Daddy, and I couldn't help but hear. Why should you bring such a man *here?*"

"There now, Connie, you mustn't bother with such things," said Cameron in a blustering tone to hide his discomfiture. "This hasn't anything to do with us . . . with us alone. And it's business, sweet." He tried to smile.

"It's a poor business, Daddy," said the girl with spirit. "It's a terrible business. And he has something to do with us, or he wouldn't be here. Are you going to pay him all that money to . . . to do away with Blodgett?"

Cameron looked at her aghast. She had heard that, too. He spoke quickly, with a frown. "You mustn't say anything like that, Connie. This is serious. It . . . it . . . I'll tell you, but you must never breathe a word of it. It's the association that will pay for Blodgett's capture. It will save us lots of money. You know what Blodgett and his gang have done."

"Capture Blodgett?" The girl's voice was full of scorn. "That ruffian capture Blodgett? You know he intends to try to kill him,

39

and, if he does kill him, he'll probably shoot him in the back. And you . . . we . . . are helping to put up the blood money."

Something very much like a groan came from Cameron's lips. "Don't make it harder," he pleaded, dropping into a chair. "I can't help it, Connie. My hands are tied."

"It's a disgrace!" cried the girl, clenching her palms. "That's what it is, Daddy . . . a *disgrace!* I heard the racket in the bunkhouse and went out there. Oh, I didn't go in . . . except into the dining room by the door. I heard the cook muttering the name, Lennister. I've heard of Lennister. He's a low, brutal gunfighter who kills men for pay. I could see the men were scared to death of him, all except one. That new man is worth more than all the rest of them put together."

"Maybe the new man doesn't know who the other man is," Cameron was betrayed into suggesting. Then he caught himself up with a frown of disapproval. "Trenton is a fool. I hired him because I believe he knows cows. You should be able to find something around here to do besides watching the men and meddling with affairs that don't concern you." He was sorry as soon as the words were out of his mouth.

But the girl, instead of looking hurt, gazed at him coolly.

"You've told me more than once, since Mother died, that I was mistress of this ranch," she said soberly. "I won't have such a man as that Lennister here. I think his kind is the most despicable breed on earth. I'd . . . I'd have more respect for Blodgett."

Will Cameron rubbed his chin with a glimmer of admiration in his eyes. "He'll be gone tomorrow," he promised.

"Yes, gone to get Blodgett and bring him back here . . . if he can," said the girl scornfully. "I won't have it. He must get off this ranch and stay off."

Cameron removed his hat and stroked his glistening forehead with the back of his hand. He looked tired, and, if he had glanced up at that moment, he would have seen a glow of compassion in his daughter's eyes.

"He'll be gone tomorrow," he repeated in a mumble.

"He must go and stay gone," said Connie firmly, going out the door.

While her father sat at his desk, staring at the papers that littered it with unseeing eyes, she went out on the porch and down the steps. She paused irresolutely on the grass, and then walked straight toward the spot where she had seen the glow of a cigarette under the trees.

Trenton strolled out and stood before her. She scanned his face in the light of the stars as he removed his hat.

"You seem to be fond of the open air," she ventured doubtfully.

Trenton, remembering that this was the second time he had been seen walking about the trees, indulged in a light chuckle.

"I had a hunch, ma'am, that sooner or later you'd be out yourself," he said in a soft drawl. "And I do need air."

She had raised her head haughtily at his first speech, but as he finished she looked at him with interest.

"I suppose it is close in the bunkhouse," she observed.

"Jammed," he said with a queer smile. "Jammed, ma'am."

Connie puckered her pretty brows as she caught the significance of this. "I suppose I should warn you," she said earnestly. "That man you were . . . you had the trouble with is dangerous. He is a common ruffian and a professional gunfighter. It's a wonder you were not killed tonight. Did you know who he was?"

"I heard him spoken of," Trenton confessed. "At supper."

"And you weren't afraid of him?" asked the girl, surprised.

"Well . . . I was thinking of my bunk. When a man hires out with an outfit and throws his bundle into a vacant bunk, it's usually understood that bunk is his." He threw away his cigarette and ground out its fire with his heel.

Connie was staring incredulously. "You risked your life with that killer for a little thing like a bunk?"

"*My* bunk," he said stoutly.

"Aren't you afraid of him?" Connie was more interested than she had ever been in a new hand on the Triangle.

"Why . . . I suppose I am. They're all afraid of him, aren't they?"

Connie drew a deep breath. "What's your name?" she inquired.

"Trenton," he replied almost eagerly.

"Well, Mister Trenton, I can't say that I understand you. But I did wish to speak to you because you're the only man around here who doesn't seem to be afraid of that . . . that beast."

"Thank you very much, Miss . . . Miss Cameron?"

"Yes, I'm Miss Cameron." The girl said it rather wonderingly. "I wonder if you . . . ?" She paused and looked at him seriously. Evidently she was satisfied, for she continued immediately: "I told Daddy I wouldn't have that man on the ranch . . . and I won't. He said he was leaving tomorrow. In the morning I'm going to ask Dad to send you for my horses. You're a good man with horses?"

"I've been around horses considerable," Trenton confessed modestly.

"Well, I'm going to ask him to send you for my horses. You're a new man without any regular place as yet, and you can be spared. But what I want you to do, besides getting the horses, is to watch where that Lennister goes. Would you do that for me? And report to *me* afterward?"

Trenton's eyes met hers with a joyous expression. "I couldn't ask for a better order, Miss Cameron," he said slowly.

She made as if to say more, but turned her eyes away with a little, haughty toss of her head.

"You'll get the order from Father or the foreman in the morning, Mister Trenton," she said severely, and turned away toward the house.

Trenton stood in the starlight, holding his hat in his hands, and stared after her with a queer expression until she disappeared.

CHAPTER SIX

Nothing further was heard from the gunman that night. He appeared to be sleeping when Trenton crept silently into the bunkhouse and went to bed in the dark. The new hand lay for a long time, looking at the patch of moonlight on the center of the floor, and if Connie Cameron, or her father, could have seen his expression, they would have been led to wonder more about this intrepid man who had had the audacity to dispute with the notorious gunfighter.

Trenton was up before dawn. In fact, he was the first man up in the bunkhouse, except the cook. He was followed speedily by the other hands, but Smith slept late and entered the dining room after the others had finished.

Trenton helped about the barn, but, anticipating the order to come indirectly from Connie Cameron, he maneuvered to keep out of the foreman's way until he saw him talking to Cameron. Shortly afterward the foreman told him to stay in. "The old man will tell you what to do," he explained, looking Trenton up and down.

It was not long before Cameron came to the barn, looking for him. He inspected Trenton narrowly, and with a scowl.

"You seem to have plenty of nerve," he grunted. "Good shot, too. But you needn't put your draw on display if you're going to work here. I've had two of my men killed when they ought to have known better. You got off lucky last night."

"Mebbe so," Trenton conceded.

"No maybe about it," said Cameron irritably. "Take my tip and lay off Smith. I don't want any more funerals around here than I can help. Get your horse saddled."

"My horse was ready before breakfast," said Trenton simply.

Cameron nodded in appreciation. "Good start," he observed. "My daughter wants her horses driven in from the east pasture. There's five of 'em. Put 'em in one of the corrals behind the big barn . . . this barn . . . out there." He pointed through the rear door of the barn.

"The east pasture?" said Trenton.

"Straight east," Cameron directed, pointing past the front of the house. "Ride down to the trees along the river and you'll find a road going east below the fields. It's the only pasture out there, and it's fenced." He frowned and looked hard at his new hand. "There's something else," he confided, somewhat mysteriously.

"I'm here for orders," said Trenton cheerfully.

"Yes, you seem to be willing enough," said Cameron, looking about as if to make sure he was not being overheard. "That fellow you had the run-in with last night," he said in a lower voice, "he'll be leaving here this morning. I was thinking you might keep along close to the trees down there, and, when he sets out, you might notice what direction he takes and perhaps keep him in sight for a while so as to make sure. Understand?"

Trenton nodded with a sly smile. It was virtually the same information that was sought by the girl. "And report to you?" he suggested.

"And report to me," Cameron affirmed. "That's right. It wouldn't hurt if he . . . if Smith didn't see you, eh? You needn't mention the matter to anybody. I'm just curious, understand?"

"Sure," said Trenton heartily. "I understand."

"I noticed when you rode in yesterday you had what looked like a pretty good horse," Cameron remarked.

"He's for sale," Trenton volunteered.

"Yes?" Cameron seemed surprised. "Wouldn't hardly think you'd want to sell that horse, if it's as good as it looks."

Trenton turned back into the barn. "I'll let him go for ten thousand," he drawled over his shoulder.

Cameron started and stared after him. Funny he would mention that particular sum. It was the very sum demanded by Lennister—by Smith for his services. But pshaw. It was Trenton's facetious way of telling him that he wouldn't sell his mount. Of course.

The courtyard—or space between the house, barn, bunkhouse, and tool shop—was deserted. The only sound, save for the rustle of the morning breeze in the cottonwoods and the stamping of horses in the barn, came from the kitchen of the house, where Connie was singing softly as she helped the housekeeper and cook.

The men who were staying at the home ranch had gone out to attend to the branding, or to their work in the fields. All of the messengers had gone, some of them leaving the night before, and there were only three or four yet to report—men who had been sent the longest distances. Cameron had dispatched a note to Sam Butler concerning the money to be paid Smith.

Cameron saw the gunman lounging in the open door of the bunkhouse, smoking a cigarette. His dislike of the man had increased steadily since the conversation with Connie the night before. He was anxious for him to be off, and he didn't care whether he ever came back or not. For Cameron had sickened of the business. Much as he wanted to see Bolt Blodgett well out of the Blue Dome country, one way or the other, he felt that if he had the thing to do over, he would not recommend the drastic measure he had advocated, and for which he could not shake off the feeling of personal responsibility.

Smith beckoned to him imperiously, a thing that did not

improve Cameron's temper as he approached the gunman.

"Thought you'd be starting out," he hinted. "Your horse has been well looked after."

Smith's eyes danced with fire for a moment. "Oh, I'll be going soon enough," he retorted. "You going to make arrangements about the money like I said? This isn't kid's play, Cameron. I want to know where I stand."

Cameron clamped his teeth over his lower lip in vexation. But he had to go through with the thing. Perhaps the gunman would never come back. Suppose he showed up with Blodgett's dead body across the front of his saddle? Cameron shuddered involuntarily. Why didn't Butler, or some of the others, come around?

"I'll attend to the money," he said sharply. "Only, for heaven's sake, get started."

Smith threw his cigarette away and, leering at Cameron, started for the barn as Trenton rode out the rear door and took a path, between the lower field and the yard, for the river.

Trenton looked back as he reached the trees along the bank of the stream and immediately checked his horse with a low whistle of surprise. He squinted at the brilliant sky as he watched a number of horsemen come galloping along the rim of the bench above the bluffs that protected the bottom land. There were six of them, well mounted and armed, with carbines slung from their saddles as well as six-shooters.

As they turned into the road and came thundering down toward the ranch buildings, Trenton drove in his spurs, cut through a small grove of trees to the lower end of the sloping yard, and from there into the cottonwoods. He rode up the line of trees with the house screening him from the visitors. When he reached a stand of golden willows at the east side of the yard before the house, he dismounted, left his horse behind the willows, and stole across the intervening space to the lower end of the verandah.

He had no sooner got there than he heard the horses of the riders in the courtyard and the sound of voices.

Connie Cameron came out on the porch without warning and saw him creeping along below the railing for a peep into the courtyard. He stopped and stared. She put a finger to her lips and came to the edge of the verandah. Leaning over, she whispered to him: "It's Sheriff Strang. I can't see why he should come here, unless . . . I wonder what he wants?"

Words reached their ears on the light wind.

"I tell you I know Lennister is here and I want him, Cameron!" The voice was high-pitched and quivering with earnest passion. "I told you I wouldn't stand for you people importing a gunman, and I won't. I'll keep my word. I heard all about it. You can't keep a thing like that quiet in this country. It means more trouble, that's all. Lennister can't stay here while I'm sheriff, and I'm sheriff for a year yet . . . don't forget that."

"It's Strang talking," said Connie in an undertone. "I . . . I hope he gets him."

They moved forward for a look into the courtyard, the girl walking on the porch and Trenton stealing along below on the grass.

As Trenton peered around the corner, he saw the riders grouped about Cameron, who was looking sternly at a man in the foreground. It was evident that this man was the one who had been speaking—the sheriff. The others had drawn their carbines from their scabbards and were holding them in readiness, their glances roving about the buildings around the courtyard.

"What makes you think he's here?" asked Cameron, who had been taken completely by surprise.

"He came here last night," the sheriff retorted, with a dark frown. "You're not denying that, are you? I know you wouldn't lie, Cameron. Has he gone?"

Trenton grinned up at the girl, who was visibly excited and who looked very beautiful in the stress of her emotion. Some of the men went into town and talked, he thought to himself. A few drinks of liquor and the whispered secret had sped as though on invisible wings, likely. Of course, it would reach the sheriff's ears. And he hadn't lost any time. The men with him were tough-looking individuals, too.

"I won't lie, as you say, Sheriff, so I won't answer any questions, either," said Cameron firmly.

"Then we'll search the place!" shouted the sheriff, whirling his horse and waving a hand to his deputies before he dismounted.

The men scattered, some to the barn, others to the outbuildings; one started toward the kitchen door of the house, but Cameron stopped him. "It isn't necessary to go in there," he said sharply.

Sheriff Strang looked from the man to Cameron, and then motioned the man away. "We won't search the house," he said, and moved toward the bunkhouse.

At this moment there came shouts from the barn followed instantly by the crack of a pistol. Cameron, the sheriff, and the deputy started on the run in that direction. Trenton, boldly leaving his place of concealment, saw a horse and rider streak across his line of vision below the barn. The gunman was making for the river.

Trenton bolted for the willows and flung himself into the saddle. He spurred his horse down the yard with the echoes of smashing reports ringing in his ears. The deputies were using their carbines. It seemed an act of utter folly for the gunman to attempt flight in the face of such fire. He had heard the loud voice of the sheriff in the barn, of course. But he might better have submitted to capture and trusted to the influence of the association to obtain his release. The sheriff could hardly prefer a charge. The sheriff really had no right to permit his men to fire at the fugitive, but Strang had evidently lost hold of himself.

Then Trenton saw that the gunman was not such a fool as might have been supposed. He had dashed in zigzag fashion to the clump of trees at the lower end of the yard and gained it. Trenton's eyes had glistened with admiration at sight of the man's horse. It was a superb animal.

A sharp report came from the trees, and Trenton swerved to the left instantly, with a startled exclamation. Four of the sheriff's men were bearing down from the other side of the house, but Smith hadn't fired at them. He had fired at Trenton! Trenton had heard the stinging whine of the bullet close to his right ear. In another moment he was in the cottonwoods and circling to get a view of the gunman as he broke for the timber along the river.

Men were running from the fields, attracted by the sounds of the shots. The deputies were pouring lead into the clump of trees where Smith had disappeared as fast as they could work the levers of their carbines. Then Trenton saw the gunman burst through the shelter and dash down the short slope toward the river. He cut to the east of him and gained the trees on the bank almost at the same moment the other reached them. The deputies came racing behind, and from the direction of the house Strang could be heard roaring orders that were unintelligible.

Trenton pushed through the trees to the water's edge and kept a sharp look-out for the fugitive. He could see some little distance up and down the river, but did not catch sight of Smith. Nor did he hear the splashing of water farther up, which would indicate that the man was crossing the stream.

In a remarkably short time the deputies were among the trees. Some crossed the river. They were joined, a few minutes later, by the sheriff and Cameron, the barn man, and others from the ranch who had come in, quickly bridled available horses, and ridden down bareback.

Trenton's intention had been to keep an eye on the gunman, as he had been instructed. But this did not seem feasible now. Shouts soon told him it would not be necessary. The fugitive had attempted to hide, and had been discovered.

Trenton rode upstream where the shouts and a scattering volley of shots indicated that Smith had been surrounded. He came into a small, partially cleared space on a high bank and saw men standing with carbines to their shoulders, covering someone below. Looking over the bank, he saw the gunman, in the water under the cutbank, waving his arms frantically. Even as he looked, Smith seemed to go deeper into the water.

"He's in quicksand, you fools!" Trenton shouted, and dismounted quickly. He took the rope from his saddle, swung the noose clear, and sent it hurtling down upon the fugitive.

"Put it under your arms!" he called. But the order was not needed, for the gunman proceeded to do so with as much haste as he could command.

His face was ashen with the fear men have of the most terrible of all deaths. He looked up and croaked: "Pull!"

Two of the deputies lent a hand to Trenton, and slowly the sucking sands released their prey. They drew him up, hand over hand, at the end of the rope, and Sheriff Strang leaned over and relieved him of his guns as he came even with the top of the cutbank.

The prisoner stood at last on the firm ground, shaking and wiping the beads of cold perspiration from his face and forehead with trembling hands.

"You're under arrest, Lennister," said the sheriff as the man looked at him with a vacant expression.

"Have you thought of the charge, Sheriff?" asked Cameron, who came up as Strang spoke.

The sheriff snapped on the handcuffs and nodded to Cameron grimly. "You heard that first shot," he said. "He dropped one of my men out of the saddle first crack. If the charge isn't murder, it'll be assault with intent to kill, and I guess that'll hold him."

Trenton caught Cameron's eye as the stockman turned away, and he could have sworn that Cameron looked more relieved than angry.

CHAPTER SEVEN

Two of the men brought Smith's horse from under the cutbank, where he had hidden the animal. A single step too far out from the overhanging bank had sent the man into the deadly quicksand, and his screams for help had speedily revealed his predicament and frustrated his ruse.

He remained silent, but his eyes lost their look of fear and began to glitter with malice as Sheriff Strang marched him afoot out of the trees and up the sloping yard to the house.

Trenton rode up with the others, keeping in the background. He saw Connie Cameron come out on the porch and caught a flashing smile of satisfaction from her as they went into the courtyard.

The manacled gunman was held in the bunkhouse while the sheriff and Cameron looked after the man who had been shot. He was found to be wounded in the right side, and the stockman shook his head dubiously as he helped the cook to wash the wound and apply a bandage. When the injured deputy had been attended to, Cameron ordered him taken into the house.

"I'll send the doctor out from town," said Strang, very business-like. "And if he thinks he can be moved, he can bring him back to Ransford in his buckboard."

"He can stay here as long as necessary, Sheriff . . . we'll look after him." Cameron's tone was free from irritation or rancor.

The sheriff looked at him sharply. "Of course you understand, Cameron, that I am doing my duty as I see it. The fact that

Lennister shot first, and without warning, doesn't look very good for him. I knew there was sure to be trouble if he was brought in here. You can't depend on a man of that kind."

"Maybe you're right," the stockman conceded. "I'm not going to try and defend him for shooting one of your men."

"I'm glad of that," said Strang. "And now I'm going to take Lennister in."

As the sheriff started for the bunkhouse to get his prisoner, Cameron hesitated. Finally, shrugging his shoulders, he followed. He waited at the door until Strang came out with the gunman. The latter's eyes were darting venom, and he fixed Cameron with a vicious stare.

"I want to talk to you a minute," he snarled out. A man rode up with Smith's horse. "Get up there," Strang commanded.

But the prisoner continued to glare at Cameron narrowly.

"Just a minute," said Cameron. "I'll hear what he has to say."

He drew aside with Smith while the sheriff watched them with a scowl and held his gun in readiness lest the prisoner attempt to break.

"You got me into this," the gunman hissed at Cameron. "How was I to know what this bunch was up to? I had my work to do, an' you told me to start. I didn't intend to hit that feller. I was trying to scare him off. You sent for me, and it's up to your crowd to get me out of this. If you're any kind of a man, you'll think that over."

Cameron opened his mouth to reply angrily, but he didn't say what was on the tip of his tongue. He merely looked at the sheriff and strode away toward the house. A few minutes later Strang and his men were riding up the bench road with their prisoner.

Trenton started for the east pasture to get Connie Cameron's horses. His face was thoughtful, and he kept looking back with a puzzled expression. When he was out of sight of the house, he pulled his horse down to a walk, and his brows were puckered in concentration. He was so preoccupied with his thoughts that he did not realize he had reached the pasture fence until his horse stopped before the gate.

Meanwhile Connie had run to her father, when he had come up on the verandah, had thrown her arms about his neck, had kissed him, and told him she was glad—for his sake. But he had shaken her off, almost roughly, and had gone into his office and shut the door.

There he flung his hat on the table and sat down at his desk, running his fingers through his hair and frowning deeply. What Lennister, the gunman, had said had hit home. He had sent for the man; he had been mainly responsible for his coming; in fact, he had been the first to hint of the advisability of taking such a course. Was he not, then, partly responsible for the events of the morning? For the shooting of the deputy?

Bolt Blodgett's crimes were forgotten as Cameron groaned with remorse, and bit his lower lip with vexation. Someone had talked in town, of course. Strang had lost no time. Doing what he thought was his duty—the fool. Cameron had sent a note to Butler, treasurer of the association, explaining the gunman's demands. Well, Butler, if he had gone into town that morning for the money, would hear of the sheriff's action and return the money to the bank. Then he would come to the Triangle and accuse Cameron of making a mess of things. Cameron wondered vaguely how the Musselshell association had handled the gunman. He could not determine just how he had failed. If Lennister had set out early that morning, if whoever had talked in town had kept still, if the sheriff had been a few minutes later. . . .

The stockman's thoughts were interrupted by a knock on the office door.

"Come in," he invited gruffly.

55

The door opened and Rounce stood, hesitating, staring at Cameron out of fishy eyes.

Instantly all of Cameron's anger returned. This rancher from the east end of the range was the only one who had dared oppose him. Now it looked as if he was the only one who had had any real sense in the matter. Spineless. Afraid.

"What do you want, Rounce?" Cameron demanded without rising from his chair.

"I thought I'd ask if . . . ?"

"If our man had showed up, eh?" Cameron interrupted, in a rage. "Want to know all about it, eh? Well, he showed up last night. And the sheriff showed up this morning and thought he could take him in without a murmur. Now one of the sheriff's men is in bed upstairs with a bullet hole in his side, and our man is on his way to jail. So you've got all the news. And it won't cost you a cent," the Triangle owner added bitterly.

Rounce fussed with the brim of his hat nervously and his gaze wavered. "I was afraid," he said weakly, "I was afraid. . . ."

"Sure you were afraid!" thundered Cameron. "That's the trouble with you pikers on the east end. You're too danged afraid to call your soul your own."

Rounce backed out the door. "We have to be careful out there," he mumbled, and turned away.

"Careful," snorted Cameron to the empty air. "And him without enough cattle to wad a shotgun," he fumed. "He'll rub it into me every chance he gets, confound him." But as his anger wore off, Cameron regretted his words to Rounce. He went out to speak to him again, but Rounce had gone.

It was shortly after he reached the pasture fence that Trenton saw a man riding east. This was Rounce, returning from his brief visit to Cameron. Trenton, studying the dejected figure in the saddle, saw the rider straighten suddenly when he left the eastern boundary of the ranch and drive in his spurs.

Trenton closed the pasture gate and, without paying further attention to the horses, rode along the line of trees close to the riverbank, keeping the horseman ahead in sight.

As the rider left the Triangle behind, he increased his pace until Trenton muttered to himself in astonishment. The man's horse had none of the appearances of a racer, yet the animal was running like one, and Trenton's own splendid bay had to extend itself.

The horseman veered into the southwest far ahead of Trenton, who kept well back to avoid being seen, and eventually disappeared in the brakes along the river.

Trenton rode on leisurely until he reached the spot where he thought the rider had vanished. Off to the north he saw a straggling band of cattle and some dilapidated ranch buildings. There was a fence, too, sadly in need of repair. It was not a prosperous-looking locality, and here the real badlands of the river began in earnest.

He pushed forward slowly, looking for a trail that the rider might have taken to enter the wild region along the river. He finally found one and turned into the badlands. For more than an hour he followed it, as there were fresh tracks upon it. Then he came to an intersection where there were other fresh tracks of cattle and unshod horses. These tracks seemingly led in all directions, and Trenton scowled as he rode for a distance on each trail in an effort to pick up the tracks left by the rider's horse.

Finally he found what he was looking for and rode deeper into the badlands. He had to proceed slowly, for there were many intersecting trails and dim paths—the tumbled locality was virtually a labyrinth. Then, in the late afternoon, he came to a clearing where there was a cluster of small cabins.

He held back within the shelter of the scrub pines and buckbrush and inspected the cabins and clearing. Several horses were grazing on the sparse grass, but there was no sign of human habitation. No smoke lifted from the chimneys of the cabins, and, as the sun sank swiftly behind the western mountains, no lights showed in any of the windows.

"Nobody home, I reckon," muttered Trenton to himself. "I better beat it back or I won't be able to find my way out tonight."

He turned back and rode as swiftly as possible for the north edge of the badlands, taking any trail that led in that direction, using the crimson fires of the sunset as a compass.

The twilight had fallen and the first stars were out when he gained the open prairie north of the badlands. He rode at a canter along the line of trees and suddenly swung his horse closer into the shadow as a band of horsemen swept across his field of vision in the north. They were riding furiously westward.

"Now what?" exclaimed Trenton aloud. "Maybe that *hombre* I was following found his friends. Anyway. . . ." He didn't finish, but put the spurs to his mount and dashed in pursuit.

The bay horse had not been ridden hard that day, and its powers of speed and endurance were now asserted. Trenton had no trouble in keeping the riders in sight. They swung far north of the Triangle ranch buildings and then raced into the northwest. But as soon as they were well off the Triangle range, they slowed their pace almost to a walk.

If one could have seen Trenton's face in the dim light of the stars, he would have marveled at the transformation from his look of that morning. The eyes were sparkling with fire, the corners of the lips drawn down slightly, and his whole expression one of mingled contempt, satisfaction, and alertness. It was a peculiar look for one so young—a look that would cause one to revise his opinion concerning his age.

As the night wore on, the riders ahead increased their pace. Finally the cottonwoods that screened the town of Ransford came into view—a deep shadow dead ahead.

Trenton turned into the cottonwoods below the riders. Two or three dim lights shone through the trees. His horse crossed the little stream almost noiselessly. He saw the riders dismounting in the shadow of the trees and saw, just beyond, what appeared to be a stone wall.

He chuckled inaudibly. "A jail raid," he breathed in a loud whisper as he got down from his horse and tethered the animal.

Then he crept along the trees toward the moving shadows ahead.

CHAPTER EIGHT

Trenton had to make a detour among the trees when he reached the spot where the riders had left their horses. One of the riders had remained with them, and they were bunched just at the edge of the trees, within easy running distance of the jail. Trenton estimated that there were at least twelve in the party, and it was all too apparent from their actions that they intended to storm the jail. He crept through the trees and reached a point where he could see the lights in the two windows in the front of the stone structure that held the captured gunman.

The jail was at the upper end of the street, and there were no buildings between it and the grove of cottonwoods along the creek. The street was deserted for its entire length. Only one or two beams of light falling across the dusty thoroughfare betrayed the resorts that remained open at that early hour of the morning. Trenton slipped into the shadow of the darkened building across from the front of the jail.

But, although the town appeared quiet and asleep, Sheriff Strang was in the jail office. He had brought the gunman in, lodged him in a cell, and had sent the doctor to the Triangle to see what could be done for the wounded deputy. He had spent the balance of the afternoon consulting with the county attorney. After supper he had endeavored to talk to the prisoner, only to receive in reply snarls and threats and abuse.

"Most vicious character I ever met," he had confided to his jailer later in the evening. "I as much as told Cameron and the rest of 'em what they could expect . . . importing a killer."

Now, long after midnight, Strang sat at his desk, his hat pulled over his eyes, considering the remarkable nature of the whole affair and awaiting the return of the doctor from the Triangle.

Must be pretty bad, he thought to himself, *for the doc to be staying out there so long. Trying to get the bullet, maybe . . . or it may be worse.* "If my man dies, it's plain, out-and-out murder!" he exclaimed aloud, slamming a fist on the desk and looking at the jailer, who was nodding in his chair.

At that instant a form appeared in the doorway. Both Strang and the jailer started up. Neither had heard the door open, it had been done so stealthily.

"Blodgett!" cried Strang, leaping from his chair as if he had been on springs. "Blodgett, by the powers. . . ."

"Don't make so much noise!" came the stern command in a hard, cold voice from the huge, swarthy-faced man who had stepped into the room. "You know me, eh?" This with a sneer. "Then you'll know what to do when I tell you."

Three men entered behind the outlaw leader, and the door was closed again.

The jailer's tipped chair had come down with a bang, and his hands had gone above his head as if by instinct. His jaw dropped, and he stared at the rustler chief in frightened fascination.

Strang's face was pale, but his narrowed eyes were darting red. Blodgett had not drawn his gun, but Strang made no effort to go for his weapon.

"What do you want?" he demanded.

"I've come for Cameron's gunman," Blodgett announced coolly.

"Yes? What do you want with him?" Strang evidently sensed it would be futile to deny the prisoner's presence or identity.

"I ain't decided," said Blodgett with a scowl. "I'll take him along an' look him over. Trot him out. Maybe I'll spank him an' give him back to you."

The men behind the leader laughed sneeringly. "Tie his hair up in ribbons," one of them suggested.

"You can't have him," said Strang.

"Trot him out!" thundered Blodgett, taking a belligerent step toward the sheriff. "Do you hand him over, or do I take him?"

"You can't. . . ." Strang paused, and his face flushed an angry red as Blodgett whirled on the jailer, grasped him by the neck, and threw him out of his chair to the floor.

"Get up an' open that cell!" commanded the outlaw.

Strang's hand darted bravely to his gun, but Blodgett's weapon appeared in his hand like magic.

"You want it?" he snarled, thrusting his jaw out and baring his lower teeth. "You goin' to keep your tongue in your head an' your hands still, or do you want it?"

The sheriff's hands came up slowly as he realized that he did not have a ghost of a chance with this gun expert who would kill in the wink of an eye. In fact, he surmised that the only reason Blodgett hadn't shot was due to the fact that the bandit hesitated at killing an officer of his importance. That would mean months of pursuit. He would have to leave the country. But he knew, too, that Blodgett would kill him if he had to.

"Go in with him an' get that wonder of Cameron's," Blodgett told one of his men, motioning to the jailer to go ahead. "Bring him out or kill him, one of the two," roared Blodgett, his anger rising.

Then he turned to Strang with a sneer. "Funny you'd take a hand in this," he said with a suggestion of curiosity.

"Funny you'd know so much," Strang retorted, white with fury.

Blodgett seemed pleased at this. He smiled evilly. "You can't make a move that I don't know about," he boasted.

Strang regarded him thoughtfully after this, while one of the men went with the jailer into the cell room beyond the office. They returned shortly with the gunman, who looked at Blodgett's imposing figure somewhat sheepishly. His bravado had fled.

Blodgett looked at him with contempt. But he didn't speak to him. Instead, he turned to Strang.

"Give him his gun," he ordered harshly. "Hustle it up. I'm goin' to take him out in the open an' maybe try him out."

He shot another look of supreme contempt at the erstwhile prisoner. Strang opened a drawer, reached into it, and drew out a gun. It was echoed by Blodgett's weapon's sharp report, and Strang's right arm dangled to the accompaniment of Blodgett's loud laugh.

"Go pick it up," he commanded the released prisoner.

The man obeyed and stood holding it indecisively. "Put it up!" roared Blodgett. "You're comin' with me!"

Sheriff Strang, clasping his right forearm where a bullet had pierced the flesh, stared incredulously as the gunman did as he was told, and then preceded the others out of the office. Blodgett paused in the doorway and looked back at him.

"As a sheriff you're as big a joke as this feller of Cameron's," he sneered. "But don't carry the joke too far," he warned, his eyes narrowing as he left.

From across the street Trenton saw them leaving and laughed queerly. He had heard the shots and had seen others of the gang run around to the front of the jail. The reports of the guns had carried, too, to the Rodeo, which was still in operation. Men came running out and raced up the street toward the jail.

Blodgett and the others, hurrying with their prisoner for the horses, paused at the line of cottonwoods and sent a volley down the street. Their guns winked red in the dark shadow.

The sheriff appeared in the door of the jail.

It's Blodgett!" he shouted at the top of his voice. "He's got Lennister!"

The men in the street sought shelter and their guns roared in reply. But Blodgett and those with him had gained their horses and were in the saddle and away before the crowd, many of whom were deputies, could take in the situation.

Trenton hurried across toward the jail as several men came running up.

"Get that man!" cried Strang, pointing at Trenton. "He doesn't belong here!"

Trenton raised his hands above his head. "I'm with the Triangle!" he called.

The men who had run toward him paused, undecided, waiting on the sheriff to see what effect this announcement would have.

"Get that man!" shouted Strang, beside himself with rage and mortification over the loss of his prisoner and Blodgett's audacity in coming right into town to defy him.

Trenton caught a flash of white in the throng as he looked about coolly and saw a man in a white jacket and apron staring at him fixedly. He smiled at the crowd.

"I tell you I'm from the Triangle!" he called to the sheriff for the second time. "You might better be getting after Blodgett."

"How do I know who you are?" yelled Strang. "Draw down on him, some of you, and bring him in here."

But Trenton had leaped back to the corner of the jail, and his gun snapped into his hand. Every man in the crowd imagined himself covered as that gun swung up at Trenton's hip.

"You're after the wrong man, Sheriff," sang Trenton as he dodged around the corner of the building.

He dashed to the rear and down toward the trees below the jail. Shouts came from the street as the deputies in the crowd started in pursuit. Trenton sped swiftly through the shadows, and the air trembled with the reports of guns. Red flashes streaked in the shadow of the jail and bullets whined past him. Then he gained the shelter of the trees.

He could hear the sheriff roaring orders as he quickly made his way to his horse. There was a rattle of harness and the creak of a buckboard from the road—the doctor returning from the Triangle. In another few moments he was riding through the creek. When he burst through the trees on the other side, he saw a swift-moving shadow on the plain far to eastward. He put the spurs to his horse and galloped madly at full speed in pursuit of Blodgett and all his men.

Behind him, in Ransford, a man in a white jacket and apron was talking excitedly to Sheriff Strang, who was swinging his uninjured arm and sputtering helplessly.

CHAPTER NINE

With the departure of Rounce, Cameron returned to the house and went up to see the wounded deputy. He saw at a glance that the man was hard hit. He had lapsed into unconsciousness and had lost much blood. Connie and the housekeeper were doing all it was possible to do, and Cameron went downstairs to his office, hoping that Sheriff Strang would lose no time getting his prisoner to town and sending out the doctor.

Cameron could not shake off the feeling that he was responsible for the whole business. He could not forget the accusation of the gunman that he and the association were responsible for the mess he was in. The stockman worried the matter in his mind until noon, and then Sam Butler rode in from the Three Bar.

The association treasurer turned his horse over to a hand and came up on the verandah, where Cameron greeted him and immediately invited him into the office.

"I've got the money," Butler announced cheerfully, tossing a packet on Cameron's desk. "Ten thousand in bills. The bank said it would crimp 'em for cash, but, if we put it over, it would be worth the trouble and the money. I soon brought 'em to time."

"You . . . brought the money?" Cameron stammered.

"Sure. My man brought your note at daylight, and I hustled right into town. Took the light rig and the grays. Came back to the ranch and then rode straight down here. I had to make a trip across the river anyway, so it didn't put me out none. Why, what's the matter, Cameron?"

Cameron waved a hand and wiped his brow with his handkerchief.

"Lennister . . . is gone!" he exclaimed. "The sheriff got him this morning. He shot a deputy trying to get away and they caught him when he got mired in the quicksand. Took him in to jail him. Funny you didn't see the sheriff's outfit."

Butler was staring at Cameron as if unable to understand. "I did see an outfit south of me when I was coming back," he said wonderingly, "but I wasn't going to stop and make any investigations with all that money on me. You say . . . ?"

"Lennister got here last night," Cameron interrupted. "He demanded ten thousand in cash for the . . . the job. Wanted it here on tap any time of the day or night when he brought in Blodgett. I . . . I told him we wanted a capture, not a killing." Cameron smiled in sour fashion. "So I sent the note to you for the money. But some of the messengers must have talked in town, for Strang got wise to his being here and showed up this morning. Lennister was slow in getting out and away, and they saw him. Now one of Strang's men is upstairs with a bullet in his side and liable to die, and our gunman must be in jail by this time."

"That's Strang for you!" Butler fumed. "Always meddling! By gad, I believe we can get a better sheriff and. . . ."

"Don't know as I blame him," interrupted Cameron to the other's surprise. "This gunman is one of the meanest-looking and acting customers I ever saw. I don't see how the Musselshell association handled him or put up with him. Tell you the truth, I . . . I was glad to get rid of him. You see. . . ." He paused, removed his hat, and, seeing that Butler still looked considerably puzzled, he recited in detail everything that had happened from the time of the gunman's arrival.

"And just before Strang took him away," he concluded, "he kind of put the whole business up to me . . . to us. Said he hadn't intended to shoot that deputy, but was trying to scare him off. Said we were responsible for all the trouble, because we sent for him, and that it's up to us to get him out of it."

"The devil!" cried Butler. "He's a paid gunman, isn't he? That's his business, isn't it? Well, he should be able to take care of himself, that's all. Don't let it worry you, Cameron. He should have gone along about his business, instead of hanging around here this morning. Lucky this new man of yours . . . what's his name . . . Trenton? Lucky he wasn't bored last night. If the deputy doesn't die, maybe we can get Lennister shipped out of the country and be rid of him. Then we'll have to make terms with Blodgett, damn it."

"Strang'll probably listen to reason," said Cameron in a tone of relief. "That is, if the deputy doesn't die. The doctor ought to be here soon." He was glad of Butler's support. Butler's arguments sounded reasonable, too. It had been up to the gunman to look out for himself, and he should have gone about his business earlier. He seemed more interested in the money. . . . Cameron looked at the packet on the table with a start.

"You'll have to take that money back, Sam," he said. "We haven't any use for it now, and I don't want that much cash around."

"Put it in your safe," said Butler with a slight frown. "It'll have to stay there till I get back from across the river, day after tomorrow, unless you want to take it into town. And how about some dinner, Will? I'm getting too old to ride all day without fodder."

Cameron, with more thought for the hospitality of his house than the sum in the packet, put the money in the safe hurriedly and led the way to the dining room, where dinner was already on the table.

Butler explained during the meal that he was cutting across country to a town south of the river, where he was to look at some stock he anticipated buying, and that he would be back in two days. It was decided that the packet of bills should remain in the safe in Cameron's office until Butler returned to take charge of it.

"Might be just as well to get word to Blodgett, some way, and offer it to him as a bribe to lay off," said Cameron with a frown.

"He'd more than likely double-cross us," grumbled Butler.

Butler took his departure right after dinner, and early in the afternoon the doctor arrived. He found the wounded deputy still unconscious and worked over him the balance of the afternoon. At supper he announced that the man's condition was precarious, and he thought it necessary to remain until the immediate crisis was over.

Meanwhile Connie Cameron was concerned because Trenton did not show up at the ranch with the horses. Cameron, with all the other things he had on his mind, had forgotten Trenton for the time being. Connie rode out to the east pasture in the afternoon and saw that the horses were there, but she saw no sign of the new hand. This puzzled her, and she told her father, who declared gruffly that Trenton was probably a line rider who had beat it after getting two square meals and a night's lodging. But the stockman was puzzled, also, for Trenton had only to ask for the accommodation to get it without the necessity of pretending he was going to work. He confessed to himself that Trenton had impressed him more than he had suspected. He did not think, of course, to associate Rounce's return to the east range with Trenton. But when Trenton failed to show up at supper, Cameron was sure he had judged him unwisely, and told Connie so. But the girl shook her head thoughtfully and continued to wonder.

"I don't believe it," she told her father.

Cameron shot a queer glance at her. "What makes you so interested in one of the hands all of a sudden . . . and a new one at that?" he asked.

"I'm interested in getting my horses in," she replied with a haughty toss of her head. "But, for that matter, Trenton was the only one who showed any spunk in front of that gunman."

With this parting shot she went back to the sick room, where the doctor was watching over his patient.

Cameron paced the verandah nervously as night came. Despite Butler's assertion that it wasn't their fault, his conscience still bothered him, and he didn't want the deputy to die and thus impress a murder charge on the gunman. He didn't want the deputy to die in any event, so far as that part of it went, but he was alive to the fact that if it was merely an assault with a deadly weapon that the gunman was charged with, it would be easier to get him off and out of the country. In this way the outside world would never know of the blunder made by himself and the association in sending for the man.

It was nearly midnight when the doctor finally came down and asked that his team be hooked up for the drive back to town.

"I figure he'll come through," he told Cameron laconically. "I'll come out again tomorrow."

Cameron felt a wave of relief sweep over him, and he bade the doctor a hearty good night as the latter started for Ransford.

For some time Cameron sat in his little office. His gaze wandered continually from the green shade of the lamp to the closed door of the safe. He had not thought much about the money since Butler had gone, but now the large sum in the safe bothered him. He didn't like to have that much money on the ranch and, particularly because it was not his, it was an added responsibility. He was tempted to take it out of the safe and hide it somewhere.

"Pshaw," he grunted finally. "I'm putting more gray hairs in my head to no account over this business."

With that thought he shrugged his shoulders, blew out the light, and went to bed. It seemed as though he had been asleep but a minute when he was awakened by a rapping on his door. He rose, lit the lamp, and saw that he had slept nearly three hours. The housekeeper, who was staying up with the wounded deputy, was at his door when he opened it.

"There's a man down in front who says he has a message for you," she explained.

"All right, I'll go right down," said Cameron. He was mystified as to the message arriving at that early hour of the morning, but he was also relieved, for he had feared that the deputy had taken a turn for the worse.

He dressed hurriedly and went down to the front door. There was a man standing on the porch. The moon had come up, and Cameron caught a glimpse of a hard face in its cold, clear rays. He looked about, but could not see the man's horse. The little cluster of ranch buildings was silent. There were no lights, no sounds save the whisper of the breeze in the cottonwoods.

"You want to see me?" Cameron asked, advancing toward his visitor.

As if his words had been a signal, dark forms appeared suddenly on both sides of the porch. In a flash Cameron remembered the money in the safe. He backed hurriedly toward the door of the house.

"Don't!" came the sharp command in a hissing voice, and Cameron caught the glint of the moonlight on a gun that the man on the porch held. "If you know what's good for you, you'll hear what the chief has to say."

A large bulky man was coming up the steps.

"Put up your gun," he said gruffly to the man who was covering the stockman. "Cameron will talk to me."

Cameron stared at the newcomer with bulging eyes. "Blodgett!" he exclaimed.

"Well, you know it," snapped the outlaw. "Glad to see me?"

Cameron's powers of speech seemed to have deserted him. He studied the outlaw's coarse, cruel features in the moonlight and shivered slightly, involuntarily.

"Goin' to bump me off with a gunman, eh?" snarled Blodgett. "Sent outside for help, eh? An' the sheriff queers your play." He laughed hoarsely, without a semblance of mirth. "Didn't think I'd nerve enough to come here, did you?" he sneered.

"You've got nerve enough," Cameron conceded.

"But your gunman didn't have nerve enough to shoot me in the back on the way out here," jeered Blodgett. "I gave him the chance. I just wanted to show you an' your association what I think of 'em, so I went in an' got your gunfighter out of jail, Cameron. Got him out an' brought him back. I'm goin' to turn him over to you so you can tell him to go ahead an' finish his job." Again Blodgett laughed, and the quality of that laugh conveyed a chill to Cameron and then angered him. In that instant he knew he never would consent to the proposition to buy the outlaw off.

Blodgett stepped to the edge of the porch above the steps. "Come up here," he ordered someone.

A man came slowly up the steps. Blodgett grasped him by the arm and whirled him in front of Cameron.

"Here's your gunfighter," he hissed between his teeth. "Back to carry out his orders."

Cameron saw the hawk-like features and the great beak of a nose of the gunman Strang had captured and taken away that morning.

"Tell the association with my compliments," jeered Blodgett as he jumped off the porch.

A jarring laugh came to Cameron out of the night, and the dark forms of the rustler chief and his men vanished.

"Broke into the jail and made the sheriff give me up," the gunman was whispering. "Didn't have a chance to shoot him with all those men with him. I'll get him yet. . . ."

"Get out of here!" roared Cameron as he ran down the steps into the yard.

From below the house came the pound of hoofs as Blodgett and his followers raced for the road that led east along the river.

CHAPTER TEN

Soon after leaving Ransford well behind in his pursuit of Blodgett and his band, Trenton decided that the outlaw had too much of a start to be kept in sight without putting his horse to a severe strain after the riding of the day. He slowed his pace and turned south toward the river, keeping a sharp look-out for signs of the posse that, he expected, would leave town immediately.

But he was unaware of the fact that the sheriff had been shot in the arm and would delay pursuit until the doctor could attend to his injury, and would then lead the posse himself.

He reached the trees and proceeded eastward at a leisurely trot, secure in the knowledge that by following the river he would bring up at the Triangle ranch buildings, situated in the bottoms north of the stream. His manner was strangely cheerful, almost exultant. After a time, failing to see any indication of pursuit, he rolled a cigarette, lit it, and smoked contentedly as he rode along.

It was the dark hour before dawn when he reached the ranch and rode down the road from the bench. He secured a lantern from the front of the barn and attended to his horse, putting the bay in a stall in the rear. Then he sought the bunkhouse. He entered noiselessly so as not to disturb the men asleep there. He snapped a match into flame with a thumbnail to see if his bunk was unoccupied and glanced instinctively toward the bunk that had been occupied by the gunman the night before.

Instantly he blew out the match and stood stockstill in the center of the room. Then he stole to the door and let himself out softly.

He drew in a long breath and looked at the ranch house. There was a light burning in the little room in the front of the house that, Trenton knew, Cameron used as an office. After a few moments of hesitation Trenton crossed the courtyard and looked in the window. He saw Cameron sitting at table with his chin in his right palm. The stockman was frowning, apparently in deep thought. Trenton went around to the front and rapped lightly on the door.

When Cameron threw open the door suddenly, Trenton found himself looking into the black bore of a gun. But the stockman lowered his weapon with a grunt of surprise when he saw who had knocked.

"What do you want?" Cameron demanded angrily. "You were through here when you lit out yesterday."

"How'd our friend in the bunkhouse get back?" asked Trenton, ignoring the other's speech and manner.

Cameron choked in his effort to answer, and then he swore outright, glaring at Trenton.

"Suppose you cut out the swearing and give me a little information," said Trenton coolly. "I had reason for lighting out yesterday. I followed Blodgett and his gang into town and was there when they raided the jail and got that fellow out there. Then I sloped for the ranch."

Cameron's eyes had widened in surprise. "You followed them?"

"I followed them," mocked Trenton. "Listen, Cameron, I take it you want to put this big chief, Blodgett, out of business. As I understand it, there's a right smart heap of money in it for whoever puts it over. Do you care who does it? Can anybody make a try for the reward stake, or are you playing a favorite?"

Cameron swore again. "I'm going to chase that fellow off the ranch first thing in the morning," he declared.

"Don't do it," said Trenton slowly. "I'm going to take a hand in this game myself. If you want to get Blodgett, let that fellow Lennister, or whoever he is, stick on the job. I'm not going to repeat that, and I reckon you can make out that I'm not talking to hear the sound of my own sweet voice. You let him stick."

With this advice Trenton swung on his heel and was off the porch and gone before Cameron could recover his surprise and call him back.

Both the gunman and Trenton ate breakfast with the Triangle hands in the bunkhouse that morning at dawn. Cameron came out, looked in, caught a single warning glance from Trenton, and left more puzzled than ever. After breakfast both men saddled their horses. The gunman had regained his vicious look and threatening attitude.

"I was up against it yesterday," he told Cameron in a snarling voice when they met in the barn. "Why didn't you tell me his nibs, the sheriff, was against this play? I'll hold you to the deal, though. You got the money?"

"It's ready when you bring Blodgett in," said Cameron quietly, looking the man steadily in the eye.

The gunman seemed satisfied. He turned away with a grumble to the effect that it had better be and led out his horse.

Trenton came sauntering out as Connie Cameron entered the courtyard from the rear door of the house and looked about her.

"I'll go right down and get your horses, ma'am," he said before the girl could speak. "One of 'em jumped the fence yesterday, and I had a lot of trouble getting it back. I'll have 'em all up by this morning."

The girl directed a swift look of triumph at her father. It was as much as if she had said: "I told you so." Her father hesitated and then nodded. But before she could reply to Trenton, their attention was attracted by the swift pounding of hoofs on the bench road, and Trenton saw, for the second time, a cavalcade of riders descending in breakneck fashion, led by a man who had an arm in a sling and who he recognized, even at that distance, as Sheriff Strang.

The gunman darted into the barn out of sight as the posse came into the courtyard and formed a semicircle about Cameron, the girl, and Trenton, who stood in front of the barn door. Sheriff Strang dismounted and looked from Cameron to Trenton with a hot flush of anger on his face.

"Thought you'd fool me, didn't you, Cameron?" he asked the stockman in a hard voice.

"I don't know what you're talking about," said Cameron, nettled at the second appearance of the official and unable to keep the antagonistic note out of his voice.

"You know very well what I'm talking about," said the sheriff angrily. "I saw your hired killer in town last night, looking for a chance to pot Blodgett when he raided the jail, thinking the fellow there was your man." He glared at Trenton, who was coolly rolling a cigarette and seemingly showing no concern. "The bartender from the Rodeo recognized him," he said grimly.

"What are you talking about, Strang?" Cameron asked sharply and severely.

"What do you take me for . . . a fool?" shouted Strang. "You had him covered up pretty well, but he was recognized by a man who saw him once in the country south of the river." He pointed to Trenton with his free hand. "That man is Lennister!" he announced shrilly.

Trenton looked up at him mildly and laughed. "Sheriff, you're sure excited," he drawled.

Out of the corner of his eye he saw Connie Cameron staring at him with a different look. Then his own eyes hardened and he tossed away his cigarette.

"That man's name is Trenton," Cameron was saying in an unconvincing voice. "He's a new hand. . . ."

It was the sheriff's turn to laugh. "I'll take the word of Joe, from the Rodeo," he said, sobering. "Where'd he come from? How long has he been here? He's Lennister, all right, and too wicked a gun-thrower to be cavorting in my country. I'm . . . I warned you, Cameron."

"What do you aim to do, Sheriff?" asked Trenton.

"Do you deny that you're Lennister?" sneered Strang.

"No, I'm Lennister," was the astounding reply as the man they had known as Trenton whipped out his gun in a flash and covered the sheriff. "What did you aim to do about it, Sheriff?" The question came in a drawl, but Lennister's eyes were darting flames of steel blue through narrowed lids. His lips pressed firmly together as Connie Cameron drew away.

The sheriff paled, but his eyes did not lose their grim look of determination. "I aim to jail you or run you out of my territory," he said firmly.

Lennister's gaze was darting everywhere. The six men with Strang stared at him, shifted uneasily in their saddles, but they kept their hands well away from their guns. One look at the changed expression on the face of the man who was covering the sheriff was sufficient to convince them that here, indeed, was Lennister. Lennister's face no longer looked youthful, nor were the eyes mild. The hand that held the gun at his hip was as steady as if it had been carved of marble. His attitude resembled a half crouch; he leaned forward ever so little. It was the unmistakable posture of the gunfighter. They took the steel-blue light in his eyes to be that of the killer.

"Listen, Sheriff," said Lennister, dropping his drawl. "I want you to have this thing right. Cameron, here, didn't know who I was when I came, didn't know it until I acknowledged it just now. I could have denied it and made you prove it, but I would have lost time and . . . I'm not going to jail, Sheriff. Don't forget that . . . and don't get too free with that good arm of yours unless you want it in a sling like the other."

He backed three steps to the open door of the barn. The men with Strang were keeping their hands well up. Connie Cameron broke through them and hurried to the house without a look at Lennister.

Lennister glanced once in her direction and laughed queerly.

"There's another thing, Sheriff," said Lennister. "I'm working on my own . . . understand? I haven't been hired by anyone. If you want to make it your business, that's your look-out, but I reckon you've got sense enough not to invite any real trouble." Lennister's tone was cold as ice. "I'm warning you, Sheriff . . . don't rile me."

With that final admonition, Lennister leaped back into the barn. For several seconds Strang stood irresolutely.

It was Cameron who spoke first. "Whatever you do, Strang, don't start more trouble here," he said in a hoarse voice. "You saw the look in his eyes."

"Surround the barn!" roared Strang to his men. "I'll keep him here or take him, if it's the last thing I do. You can't put this over on me, Cameron . . . !"

His men had split into two factions of three each, and each trio had spurred their horses around the barn on either side. Strang started to draw his gun with his left hand. At that moment there came the smashing impact of flying hoofs on the board floor of the barn and a great bay horse streaked past them.

Strang succeeded in jerking out his gun and fired. There was a flash of brown at the corner of the house, and the sheriff emptied his gun at the thin air.

The posse came galloping back as Strang climbed into his

saddle. He led them around the house, and they caught a last glimpse of Lennister as he spurred his flying mount into the trees at the lower end of the yard.

Smith, the gunman, came out of the stall, where he had been hiding, with an evil grin on his face. Cameron had run toward the front of the house. Smith got his horse and rode quietly away through the trees behind the barn and then headed for the river.

On the porch Connie Cameron stood, her hands clasped against her breast, staring toward the east road as the echoes of the flying hoofs slowly died away.

Chapter Eleven

Lennister leaned forward in the saddle and spoke to the bay horse. After his dash from the barn and down the yard he scorned the steel, and his mount felt no prick of spurs. But at the sound of his master's voice, insistent and urging, the horse sped like the wind along the road that led westward just above the trees lining the banks of the river.

Looking back over his shoulder, Lennister saw the sheriff and his posse break through the trees and urge their horses in hot pursuit. They even fired at him in their excitement, but they were not in range. Lennister's face darkened and his eyes flashed fire as the echoes of the shots came to him and he saw the puffs of white that drifted from the muzzles of smoking guns.

Soon a turn in the road shut his pursuers off from view, and Lennister gave his whole attention to his horse. The animal spurted at his command, and he widened the distance between himself and the posse. For a mile or more he sped thus, and then he reached the horse pasture. But he didn't stop to open the gate in the fence that marked the eastern end of the enclosure about the ranch domain proper. He sent the bay hurtling over the wire and swerved south, close to the trees.

He still was out of sight of the posse when he turned into the trees on a thin trail and trotted his horse to the riverbank. As he had expected, he found a ford at this place and crossed the river without trouble. He went on through the trees and came out on the open prairie just south of the river. Here he turned east again and sent the bay flying along the southern edge of the trees. After fifteen minutes of fast riding he checked his pace, secure in the knowledge that he had left Strang and his men far behind. He felt that the sheriff would get tired of the futile chase when he realized that none of the horses of the posse could catch the bay. Then his thoughts strayed from the sheriff to Connie Cameron and the way she had looked at him when she learned he was Lennister. His gaze hardened again.

"Reckon we're mighty bad people," he said aloud, and his horse pricked up his ears. "And that danged fool of a sheriff called me a paid killer!"

He stared grimly ahead, and gradually his face lost its stern lines and his eyes softened until their light was almost wistful. He seemed to shake off the mood that was upon him with a shrug of his broad shoulders as he caught sight of the tumbled ridges and gnarled pines of the badlands ahead.

From this point he proceeded more cautiously, and finally he entered another trail leading to the riverbank and crossed the stream again. At the edge of the cottonwoods on the north bank he searched the plains westward for sign of Strang and his posse, but saw nothing. He trotted his horse along the line of trees till he reached the western boundary of the badlands. In the northwest, not more than a mile away, he could see the dilapidated ranch buildings he had noticed the previous afternoon. A number of horses were in a corral up there.

Lennister looked long in that direction and then turned his horse into the labyrinth of the river brakes.

The last pink ribbons of the sunset festooned the sky above the western mountains as Lennister rode slowly back the way he had come on the south side of the river that morning. His hat was pushed back and his face looked boyish in the soft light of the dying day. He appeared cheerful, for his lips were pursed and he whistled a range tune, swinging one foot clear of the stirrup. But his gaze roved continually ahead, to either side, behind.

The pink ribbons were swallowed by a sea of blue, and the first purple shades of the twilight fell athwart the land. The breeze freshened and murmured in the cottonwoods. Lennister edged in closer to the trees as their shadow slanted on the edge of the plain. In time, when it was almost dark, he came to the trail leading to the ford he had used that morning. He crossed the river, rode to the Triangle fence, put his horse over it in a swift, running jump, and turned once more to the trees—on the north bank this time.

He did not depend on the shadows screening him from the view of anyone who might be abroad, but rode into the shelter of the cottonwoods. Night came and the early stars pierced the deep-blue curtain of sky as he walked his horse through the trees close to the high bank of the river.

"Must be a ford down here somewhere," he muttered to himself. "They cross the river from the ranch, I know, but where. . . ."

His soliloquy was broken off abruptly, and he reined in his horse with an involuntary exclamation. Ahead of him was a small clearing among the trees—a fragrant meadow. There was a horse there, and a vision of white in the saddle. Lennister could just make out the profile of Connie Cameron in the faint light of the stars.

His first thought was of noiseless flight, but she had heard him. She was looking his way, and Lennister was certain she had seen him. He frowned and shook his head as if he had suddenly been brought face to face with a problem that was too much for him. Then he heard his name called softly—very gently.

"Trenton . . . Lennister?"

She had recognized his horse, of course, or did she recognize his posture in the saddle? Or? He shrugged. There was nothing for it but to ride out and meet her. He walked the bay into the meadow and swept the hat from his head.

"Miss Cameron . . . ma'am . . . I sure didn't expect to see you."

"Nor did I expect to see you, Lennister." She was looking at him searchingly, but not with the look she had given him that morning—the look of mingled horror and disappointment.

"Why have you come back?" she asked curiously.

"I reckon you wouldn't believe me, Miss Cameron . . . me being what I am," he said with a faint suggestion of sarcasm.

"Regardless of what you are, I hardly believe you would lie, Lennister, although you did say your name was Trenton," she said with a pretty frown.

"It happens to be my *first* name, ma'am," said Lennister quietly.

"Oh!" She seemed impressed by his tone. "Then I guess I can believe you. Why did you come back, Trenton Lennister?"

"I came back because I thought I might be able to do your dad a favor," he replied. "Between that impostor, Smith, as he calls himself, and that sheriff, they've come pretty close to making a dog-goned fool out of him."

Connie Cameron raised her head haughtily. "I hardly think my father needs the assistance of a . . . a . . . of yourself to retain his dignity," she said stiffly. "You must have some other reason." She looked at him with suspicion.

"Very likely I have, ma'am," he said with a queer smile and a little bow. "Men such as you take me to be hardly tell their business to any girl who asks them."

Her haughtiness melted under the reproof, and her curiosity returned.

You seem so young to be in such a . . . a business," she said in a tone of regret. "Do you . . . like it?"

"It's according to how you look at it, ma'am."

"But it's outrageous," she declared. "It's . . . why, it's infamous. A hired gunman . . . a killer. I can hardly believe it."

"I'm not hired, ma'am," he said with a smile. "I'm working for . . . Lennister."

"You call it working?" she said scornfully. "If it's legal at all, which I doubt, you're nothing more or less than a legalized murderer. How many men have you killed, Mister Lennister?"

"Three," replied Lennister without an instant's hesitation.

The girl gave a little gasp. "Well, you're frank, at least," she conceded. The look he hated had returned to her eyes. "Are you proud of it?"

"I'm tolerably glad to be alive, Miss Cameron," drawled Lennister. "I wouldn't be if those three gents I bored had had their way about it. Every last one of 'em drew first, and one of 'em . . . the worst . . . shot me in the back before I could turn around. They'd have been hung sooner or later . . . I don't shoot for fun, Miss Cameron."

Something in his tone as he spoke the last words conveyed another mild reproof. It also seemed to reveal a new side of his character, although she could not determine the nature of it.

"It seems too bad," she said, as if to herself. "You are young and able. Why can't you give up this . . . this business, as you call it?"

"I hadn't thought of it, ma'am. I've sort of been roped and tied by circumstances, I reckon. Is the sheriff still sticking around?"

"He went back this afternoon," she answered impatiently.

"And that fellow, Smith . . . is he gone, too?"

"He's disappeared," she replied with an involuntary shudder. Then she looked at Lennister's face in the starlight. "Smith looked more like what I expected you to be," she observed. "You don't *look* like a gunman, Mister Lennister."

"Thanks," said Lennister dryly. "That wounded deputy die?"

"The doctor doesn't think he'll die. You seem much interested in . . . in everything, Mister Lennister."

"I'm enough interested to ask you to keep quiet about my being around here tonight," said Lennister earnestly.

"Naturally you're afraid of being captured," she said, with a hasty look around the meadow. Then, with a subtle feeling of guilt: "You don't want me to tell my father?"

"I'd like to ask you not tell anyone, Miss Cameron," he returned humbly. "I promise you it's for the best."

She looked at him closely and shrugged. "I must be going. It's past the time when I usually end my evening ride. It might be. . . ." She hesitated and flushed slightly. "I believe you impressed Father," she said slowly. "It might be . . . if it would help you to give up your present occupation . . . that Father might find a place for you on the ranch." She got the last words out with difficulty and looked at him quickly.

Lennister was smiling. "You're a thoroughbred, Miss Cameron," he said simply.

"You wouldn't consider it, of course," she said smartly, with another flush. "I merely made the suggestion for your own good. I must be going."

"Just one more question, Miss Cameron. Is there a ford of the river near here?"

"Below the oat field, west of the house," she replied, raising her reins. "There's a road leading south of the river to the Missouri. You ought to make it tonight easy. Good bye, Lennister."

But he did not answer. He sat his horse, with his hat in his hand, as she rode away through the trees in the direction of the ranch house. Then he moved on down the river to a point just west of the house. Here he dismounted, and tied his horse in a clump of alders. Then he moved silently to a vantage point where he could watch the house, the fields below it, the road east of it, and the bench. He sat down and began his vigil.

Hours passed, and Lennister remained motionless, with his back against a tree trunk, watching. The lights in the house and in the bunkhouse went out, and a silence so complete that it seemed a living, breathing thing settled over the Triangle buildings. There was only the soft stir of the breeze in the leaves of the cottonwoods. Midnight came and passed and the moon rose and floated like a splash of silver in the sky. Finally Lennister roused himself.

A shadow was moving swiftly in the lower yard below the house. It blended with the shadow of some trees and was lost. When it emerged, it was in the form of a man stealing across the yard toward the front of the house.

Lennister rose, hitched his gun, and watched through narrowed lids as the man slipped around the farther corner of the porch and disappeared. Then Lennister stole down through the trees to the lower yard, hurried across to the grove of cottonwoods just east of the house, and crept through them until he had a view of the courtyard.

He saw the dark form of the man at a window at the side of the house near the front. He knew the window, although he could not see it. It was the window of Cameron's office. He smiled derisively as he saw the man's body slowly disappear over the sill. Then he slipped across to the corner of the porch and, foot by foot, edged around to the window. He removed his hat and peered stealthily within. A ray of moonlight fell across the face of a man. It was Smith, the impostor, kneeling before the Triangle safe, slowly turning the knob of the combination dial, feeling and listening for the telltale fall of the tumblers.

Chapter Twelve

Smith was so occupied with the delicate task of opening the safe, old-fashioned though it was, that he did not once look up at the window, and Lennister watched while the man completed the operation. At last the door of the safe swung back. Lennister drew back as Smith looked hurriedly around, and, when he next peered through the open window, the impostor was taking out a small packet.

Lennister hurried back across the lawn in front of the house to the trees, and ran through them toward the river. When he reached the big cottonwoods on the bank of the stream, he looked back and saw Smith's shadow gliding down the yard. He hurried to his horse and led the animal to the edge of the trees.

Smith passed below toward the oat field west of the house, and Lennister followed, leading his horse and keeping well in the shadow of the trees. At the corner of the field nearest the river, Smith darted into the trees. Lennister moved slowly toward the bank of the river, listening. In a short time he heard the faint splashing of water and knew that Smith was crossing the ford.

Lennister mounted and rode slowly along until he reached the road leading to the ford. He turned south and crossed the river. He sent his horse quickly up the slope of the south bank and came out of the trees. His first look was toward the east, but he saw nothing in that direction. His gaze swept southward, and he quickly made out a moving shadow speeding southward on the limitless expanse of moonlit plain.

"He's giving Blodgett the go-by!" exclaimed Lennister aloud, with an unpleasant laugh.

Then he tickled the bay with his spurs and spoke to him. The horse leaped ahead and started across the prairie at racing speed. Smith, unsuspecting, gloating, doubtless, over the theft of the $10,000 from the Triangle safe, was not keeping a strict watch on his back trail. Lennister gained rapidly before he saw the man ahead let out his horse. Then began a race southward on the plain.

Smith's nearest refuge was the brakes of the Missouri, but they were miles and miles away. He spurred his horse till the blood ran in an effort to shake off the unknown pursuer. But he couldn't shake the bay. Lennister continued to gain, slowly but surely, riding well forward in the saddle and speaking to his mount in an insistent, encouraging voice, keeping his eyes ever on the fugitive ahead.

Finally the shadow of a low butte showed dead ahead—a dark blot on the surface of the plain. Smith made for it with a last desperate burst of speed. Lennister urged the bay into a heartbreaking spurt with his spurs. There was a red flash ahead, and the bark of a gun came sharply on the wind. Lennister swerved to the right and back again, as there were more red flashes. The reports of Smith's gun seemed to thunder in his ears, and he drew his own weapon.

He was close to Smith now, and the latter's horse was giving out. Lennister waited till he could almost see his quarry's face in the moonlight. He was a little to the left of Smith. He brought his gun up and over the hand that held the reins and fired. Smith's hat went spinning from his head, and he checked his horse as if by instinct.

Lennister closed in. "Drop that gun!" he called sharply.

At the sound of his voice and a glimpse of his face in the cold light of the moon, Smith flung away his gun and reined in his winded horse. His eyes had lost their evil glint, and the vicious look was gone from his face. His gaze wavered, but he sat sullenly in the saddle as Lennister drew up beside him.

"Going to give Blodgett the slip, eh?" said Lennister in a tone of contempt. "Thought ten thousand was too good a stake to split, didn't you?"

Smith appeared surprised. "You know . . . ?" A shrewd look came into his eyes. "It wouldn't be so bad to split with just one," he suggested craftily.

"With me, for instance?"

"Why not?" said Smith eagerly.

"Smith," said Lennister slowly, as his eyes narrowed, "it galls me to think that the likes of you would have the nerve to try and palm himself off for me. If I weren't in this thing to a finish, I'd give you your gun and make you draw."

Smith's face paled, and his great beak of a nose looked like the white beak of a vulture in the moonlight. "I never told 'em outright that I was you, Lennister," he whined.

Lennister straightened in his saddle with a snort of deep disgust. "Turn that horse of yours around and start back," he ordered. "And don't talk."

It was dawn when they arrived at the Triangle and dismounted in front of the house. Will Cameron came out on the porch with a frowning look of perplexity. Lennister saw the wide eyes of Connie over his shoulder.

"Here's your impostor, Cameron," said Lennister with a deep scowl. Then to Smith: "Throw him that package of money."

He looked at Connie Cameron as Smith, with a glare of hate at all of them, threw the packet containing the $10,000 at Cameron's feet.

Cameron picked it up with a look of wonder. "Sneaked back here and touched your safe for it last night," said Lennister almost savagely. "Better put him somewhere where he'll keep till later."

The stockman started to ask a question, but Lennister interrupted him.

"Listen, Cameron," he said sharply. "I want every man in your outfit that can ride a horse and shoot a gun ready to leave here in an hour or two. All of 'em, understand? I watched this man rob your safe last night and let him start away because I thought he was going to Blodgett. But he was going to beat it south with the money on his own hook. I brought him back. That's enough to show you that I'm halfway square, anyway, and mean business. Do I get the men?"

He kept his eyes on Connie Cameron as he spoke, and his face darkened as the girl turned back into the house with a disdainful toss of her head.

"Sure you get the men," said Cameron. "But what're you going to do?"

"I'm going to get Blodgett," snapped Lennister. "And I'm not getting him on your account, either."

With a savage stare through the vacant front doorway, Lennister motioned to Smith to precede him around the house toward the barn.

After Smith had been locked in a storeroom, Cameron sent the barn man to call in the hands and notify the men who were on the north range to hurry to the house.

Within an hour the men began to arrive. In compliance with Lennister's surly demand, Cameron gave the orders for the men to secure their best mounts and arm themselves in anticipation of trouble. Lennister ate breakfast in the bunkhouse, and a meal was carried to the prisoner.

Only once did Lennister see Connie Cameron after his return. She stopped him as he was crossing the courtyard.

"I'm glad to see," she said in a superior tone, "that, since you think you've to go after Blodgett, you're going at it in a regular way."

Lennister flushed angrily at her tone. "What kind of an *hombre* do you think this Blodgett is?" he blurted.

"He's bad and he's dangerous," she said in the same voice. "But, of course, he's no match for a man of your . . . profession."

Lennister strode on without another word or look. But his face was dark and his eyes glittered ominously.

It was nearly noon when they rode away from the Triangle, with Lennister and Cameron in the lead. A backward glance showed Lennister that Connie Cameron was standing on the porch, looking after them. His jaw snapped shut with a click of his teeth, and he swept ahead.

They followed the east road to the gate, passed through, and started across the prairie north of the river. Lennister set a stiff pace, and in little more than an hour they reached the western end of the badlands. Here Lennister ordered all the men, except Cameron, to scatter among the trees and wait. He motioned to Cameron to follow him, and rode swiftly northwest toward dilapidated ranch buildings that scarred the face of the prairie.

"Why, you're heading for Rounce's place!" exclaimed Cameron in surprise.

"That his name?" said Lennister grimly. "I followed him out here the first day I went after your girl's horses."

Cameron remembered Rounce's visit the morning the sheriff took Smith into town. Lennister must have followed him when he started for home. But what had Rounce to do with it all? He looked at Lennister and saw that he was smiling—or was he sneering?

Rounce came out of the house as they dismounted at his door. He turned his faded blue eyes from one to the other in an uneasy, fishy stare. He greeted Cameron in a mumble and invited them in. As soon as they were inside the shabby room, Lennister turned on him.

"Where's Blodgett?" he demanded.

Cameron stood speechless as he heard the question and saw the pale face of Rounce go a shade whiter.

"Blodgett?" said Rounce, wetting his lips with his tongue. "Why, I . . . how should I . . . ?"

"Where is he?" said Lennister in a louder, more sinister voice.

Rounce looked at Cameron appealingly, but Cameron was scowling. It had suddenly been brought home to the stockman that Lennister knew exactly what he was doing. Here was the man—the trailer and gunfighter—who had cleaned out the rustlers in the Musselshell. It was a different man from the one who had ridden into the Triangle and had taken a job under the name of Trenton.

Lennister suddenly leaped forward and grasped Rounce by the neck.

"Talk, you rat," he said harshly, shaking the white-faced rancher until his teeth chattered. "Where's Blodgett?"

"In . . . the badlands," gasped Rounce, trying to shake himself free.

Lennister threw him backward into a chair and whirled on Cameron. "There's your association traitor," he snapped. "He told Blodgett all about your meeting in Ransford, and Blodgett sent Smith to palm himself off as me. Then this rat drifted in and found out the sheriff had grabbed Smith, and he beat it back to tell Blodgett. Next thing, Blodgett got Smith out of jail and put him back on the job so he could steal your ten thousand. Pretty scheme." He laughed shortly.

Cameron's face had darkened, and he was glaring at Rounce angrily.

"Blodgett made me," Rounce whimpered. "We never had any protection out here, an' he had me at his mercy. We . . . I . . . ," and he broke off with a whine as Cameron took a step toward him.

Lennister grasped the stockman's arm. "Let him alone," he said sharply. "It won't do the association any good to come down on this poor fool. Maybe there's something in what he says about Blodgett having him at his mercy out here. If he does what he's told, go easy with him."

Cameron remained motionless, with clenched fists. Rounce, cowering in his chair, nevertheless looked a bit hopefully at Lennister.

"Whereabouts in the badlands is Blodgett's hang-out?" Lennister demanded. "You know where he is. I did a little watching out here yesterday, and saw the whole crowd leave your place."

Rounce's lips quivered as he trembled in a nervous frenzy. Then slowly he described the spot where Lennister had seen the little group of cabins in the clearing.

"You know a straight trail there?" Lennister asked sternly.

Rounce nodded with a fearsome look at the infuriated Cameron.

"All right, get your horse," commanded Lennister.

A few minutes later Rounce, hunched and dejected in the saddle, was leading the way toward the place where the Triangle men were waiting.

CHAPTER THIRTEEN

Rounce *did* know a shorter trail to the rendezvous of the outlaws than the one, or several, Lennister had taken the day he went in there. He led the Triangle outfit almost in a straight line southeast, and Lennister saw that the trail was well covered and apparently but little used. Doubtless Blodgett and his men took devious routes to cover up their tracks. Lennister knew that in his case he had merely blundered into the place.

As they proceeded, Rounce became more and more cheerful. He lost his dejected air, and hope glimmered in his eyes.

"I'll be glad to get . . . rid of Blodgett," he confided to Lennister with some hesitation. "I was . . . afraid of him. But maybe you won't get him."

"I'll get him or I don't know his kind," said Lennister grimly. "Remember, now, we want to slow up this side of the place and surround it."

Rounce nodded and looked timidly back at Cameron, who took no notice of him whatsoever.

In about half an hour Rounce called softly but excitedly to Lennister: "We're getting close."

Lennister called a halt and compelled Rounce to explain in detail how the place could be surrounded. Rounce pointed out the trails leading from that point to the north and south of the rendezvous.

"But you can't get in east of it, for there's a big quicksand soap hole there," he explained. "I'm afraid . . . I'm afraid he'll get away."

Lennister dispatched a number of men to approach the rendezvous from the north and south, and then sat his horse, frowning, in deep thought. There were thirty-two in the attacking party all told. From what he had seen and had gotten out of Rounce, there were not more than fifteen, or eighteen at the most, of the rustlers in the outlaw rendezvous. They were waiting for Smith, according to Rounce, before conducting another raid on the cattle on the north range. Blodgett had been in a fury the day before and had accused Smith of bungling. He did not know, of course, of the presence of Lennister on the Triangle.

"I reckon Blodgett'd better know about Smith," said Lennister finally, with a keen look at Rounce. "And I reckon it's up to you to go in and tell him."

Rounce cowered back. "He'd shoot me when you attacked," he said in terror. "I can't go in there . . . now."

"Blodgett's got to know about Smith, and most of all where Smith is and how he tried to get away with that money," said Lennister with conviction. "Listen to me, Rounce." He fixed the frightened rancher with a stern gaze and quickly told him about what had happened early that morning. "Blodgett'll be too much obliged to you for the news to think of anything else," he finished. "Tell him you were in to the ranch and found out . . . tell him anything. Then beat it out of there, and, when you leave, we'll go in. Perk up, Rounce . . . you're going in with the message. If you get the word to him privately, I don't think you'll have to worry about him any more. But if you tell him anything except what I've told you to say, you'll have to worry about *me!*"

Rounce looked about helplessly. "You're sure . . . you'll give me a chance to get out?"

"I keep *all* my promises," said Lennister in a tone that made Rounce shiver.

But the rancher got hold of himself and finally rode on down

the trail. Lennister and Cameron climbed a ridge from where they had a view of the rendezvous. There were a score of horses in the clearing, and smoke was issuing from the chimneys of several of the cabins.

They saw Rounce ride boldly into the clearing. He was accompanied by another man, who they assumed to be the lookout on the trail. Rounce rode directly to one of the cabins, dismounted, and vanished inside. After some little time they saw Rounce come out and mount hurriedly. He was followed by a big man whose voice carried to the top of the ridges as he shouted an indistinct order. Rounce spurred his horse across the clearing and rode as fast as he could.

Lennister ran down the ridge, followed by Cameron, and threw himself into the saddle. Instantly the Triangle outfit was in action, riding madly down the trail. As they burst out into the clearing, they saw men running for the horses. The band was out of the cabins and scattered. The Triangle men, with wild yells, began shooting. From the north and south sides of the clearing other Triangle men came upon the scene.

A few of the outlaws had secured their horses and were mounted bareback, clinging to halters, swinging smoking guns towards the attackers. The dust rose in clouds and swept over the fighting cowpunchers and rustlers. Riderless horses dashed in and out among the combatants and soon Lennister's voice was heard roaring above the confusion of sound.

"Get out of the dust! Keep 'em surrounded!"

The Triangle men swept toward the edges of the clearing, where the air was clear. Then, as the dust settled somewhat, the outlaws tried to break through and were met by a withering volley. A breath of wind sent the dust flying southward, and several of the followers of Blodgett were seen sitting their horses, holding their hands aloft. Others, confused by their sudden exposure and bewildered by the unexpected attack, followed their

example. Half a dozen men were lying on the ground, wo
or fatally shot. The Triangle men closed in about them w
cheer.

Lennister dashed for the cabin he had seen Rounce enter. I
flung himself from his horse, crept around the corner to the
door, and leaped inside. The cabin was empty. He came out
calling orders.

"Search the cabins!"

He had seen by swift glances that Blodgett was not among
the men who had surrendered, nor was he on the ground.
Several of the Triangle outfit helped him search the cabins. Two
men were found who gave themselves up, but there was no sign
of Blodgett to be seen anywhere.

Lennister rode to where Cameron was directing his men in
the work of disarming and securing the prisoners.

"Lost three men," Cameron began, "and . . . did you find
Blodgett?"

"Bring in the prisoners," snapped Lennister, paying no heed
to the question. Then he spurred his horse across the clearing at
breakneck speed and disappeared where the trail entered the
trees.

It was late in the afternoon when Connie Cameron heard a
heavy step on the verandah. She hurried out, thinking that her
father and the others had returned to the deserted ranch. But
the bulky form framed in the front doorway, the coarse, evil
features and the glittering black eyes caused her expression to
change instantly from one of hopeful expectancy to stark fear.
She had heard Bolt Blodgett described enough times to
recognize him at first sight.

Blodgett came in boldly. The girl was unable to move or
speak. He grasped her rudely by the arm and dragged her out
on the verandah.

"Where's that man they've got penned up here?" he demanded hoarsely. "Where is he, I say?" He twisted her arm until she found her voice and cried out in pain.

"He's . . . in . . . the barn storeroom," she managed to say, her eyes wide with fear and resentment.

"Show me," the outlaw ordered. "Hurry up!" He flung her down the steps, and unable to help herself or recover in any measure from the shock of his appearance, she led the way in a daze to the barn and pointed to the padlocked door of the storeroom where Smith was confined.

Blodgett looked about with bloodshot eyes, and his gaze fell on a pick near the barn door. In another few moments he had shattered the lock and flung open the door.

"Come out here!" he ordered in a queer, croaking voice as his lips pressed together.

The girl's hands flew to her breast as she saw the white, cowering face of Smith. The man staggered out of the door, blinking in the light, and backed against the wall.

"Goin' to double-cross me, eh?" Blodgett's tone was terrible. But it was as nothing compared to the look in his eyes. "Was that it?" he thundered furiously.

"I . . . no. . . ." Smith's tongue froze to the roof of his mouth.

Then Blodgett laughed, and the laugh was drowned in the roar of his gun. Smith pitched forward on his face, clawing at the air. Blodgett whirled on the horrified girl.

"Make for the house," he commanded. "You saw *that.* . . ." And he pointed at the still form of Smith. "Do as I say an' you'll be all right."

He took her by the arm and walked her to the front of the house, across the porch and into the little office.

"Open that safe," he snarled, pointing to the door of the Triangle's cash box. "You've got the combination," he continued harshly. "Your old man tells you everything. Open it!" His hand dropped to the butt of his gun, and the girl kneeled down in a daze before the safe and proceeded to open it with trembling fingers.

Blodgett found the packet of money readily and stuffed it into a pocket with a gleam of satisfaction in his eyes. Connie had backed to the door. She heard another step upon the porch, a lighter step, and a great fear clutched at her throat. She tried to cry out, but Blodgett threw her out of his way on the instant. She fell to the floor of the hall, and, looking up, saw Lennister standing at the top of the steps. Then her view of him was blotted out by the huge form of Blodgett.

For what seemed an age, there was silence. Then: "Put 'em up, Blodgett."

It was Lennister's voice, ringing, stern, and clear.

"Lennister!" yelled Blodgett.

The outlaw's right hand moved like lightning and a gun barked sharply.

Connie had closed her eyes, and, when she opened them, they widened in surprise. Blodgett's hand, holding his gun, was at his side. Then he crumpled to the floor of the porch, and she saw a wisp of smoke curling from Lennister's hip, and his eyes, glowing with a steel-blue light, were looking into hers.

CHAPTER FOURTEEN

Four men were seated in Will Cameron's office at the Triangle.

"It was a mighty smooth piece of work," Cameron was saying, "and we owe a lot to you, Lennister."

Lennister was rolling a cigarette. "I understand you offered five thousand, all told, for breaking up the Blodgett gang," he said slowly. "That's all you owe me."

"For my part, I'd be willing to give you the ten thousand," said Sam Butler, who had just ridden in from the south.

Lennister shook his head. The youthful look had returned to his face, and there was a wistful glow in his eyes. "It wasn't the money altogether," he said mysteriously, as the other men looked at each other with puzzled expressions. He was thinking of Connie Cameron and her words and look the night before when he had met her in the meadow.

Sam Butler handed him a packet of bills. "You'll find the five thousand there," he said heartily.

"How'd you happen to come back here?" asked Sheriff Strang, who had arrived at the ranch in time to hear Cameron tell the story to Butler. "I mean, how'd you happen to come back the last time just when you did?"

Lennister looked at him quizzically. "I reckon I know something about men of Blodgett's stamp, Sheriff. If I didn't, I wouldn't be a professional special agent for cattlemen's associations." He smiled wryly and lit the cigarette. "I sent that fellow Rounce in to tell Blodgett about Smith's trying to double-cross

101

him because I knew Blodgett wouldn't be satisfied until he'd got Smith. I felt right sure that if he did get away from us there, he'd beat it for here to get even with Smith if it was the last thing he ever did. I'd clean forgotten about the money here." He paused and looked sharply at the sheriff. "I'd met Blodgett once before, south of here," he said slowly. "He . . . shot a friend of mine just as he shot Smith . . . unarmed."

The sheriff shrugged and glanced at the others. "You could have a place on my force of deputies if you wanted to stick around, I guess," he suggested.

Lennister laughed. "And stagnate in your stuffy little jail office? It isn't in the pictures, Sheriff."

Strang frowned. "If a gunfighter is going to hang out in my territory, I want him on my force," he said stubbornly, looking at Cameron and Butler. "Otherwise. . . ."

"He should move on," Lennister supplied, rising from his chair. "Well, gentlemen, when it comes to moving on, it happens I have a horse."

His eyes and smile mocked them for a single moment, and then he quickly went out.

The golden promise of another day was in the last crimson streamers of the sunset as Lennister rode into the courtyard and turned toward the road to the north bench. Connie Cameron was at the corner of the verandah.

"Mister Lennister," she called softly. Then in an unusual, impulsive voice: "Trenton!"

He drew rein and looked back, the dying light of the sunset marking his profile.

She hurried toward him. "I . . . I didn't altogether understand," she said slowly. "Blodgett . . . he . . . it was terrible. I suppose someone has to . . . maybe it *was* the only way to deal with him. You . . . you will be coming back to see us some time?"

He sat very still, and finally his words came in a voice that had lost its sharpness and its drawl.

"I reckon that would be dangerous, Miss Cameron."

"But I . . . I didn't mean for you to come in your . . . your of-ficial capacity," she said tremulously.

"Dangerous to my peace of mind, I meant, Miss Cameron," he said in a voice so low she could barely catch the words. "But if you ever want me . . . a message . . . I'll come."

She tried to speak, but could only wave her hand to show that she had heard.

Then Lennister cantered to the road that wound up the bluffs. She saw horse and rider outlined for a few moments on the rim of the bench, and then he was gone, and she was look-ing at a first brave star.

★ ★ ★ ★ ★

PART TWO

★ ★ ★ ★ ★

CHAPTER FIFTEEN

A crowd was gathering one evening, a year later, in front of the Rodeo resort. Yellow gleams of lamplight, streaming from the windows of the resort, cast a weird hue on bronzed faces and brought the sea of bobbing, broad-rimmed hats into bold relief. Men were hurrying toward the spot from up and down the short, dusty street. Strains of music came from the dance hall nearly opposite the resort. Overhead the swimming stars looked coldly down upon Ransford, nestling among the weaving cottonwoods, wildly responding to its annual Grand Decoration Day Celebration and Ball—Don't Miss It.

Evidently something not on the program was taking place in front of the Rodeo. There were loud and excited voices and harsh laughs.

"Go to it, kid, you're the boy that can do it!" cheered a lanky cowpuncher, swinging his hat.

A dark, swarthy-skinned young fellow, with an eye unnaturally bright, swung on his heels in the center of the admiring circle and scowled.

"Who said that?" he demanded, jerking off his hat as if he would throw it on the ground, roll up his silk shirt sleeves, and annihilate the speaker on the spot.

"Tear into it, Claude!" came the voice from somewhere in the throng. "The Bar Cross is a dozen strong behind you!"

The youth peered about with a menacing look, returned his hat to his head, swayed just enough so that one could notice it, and then spoke again.

"I don't need no dozen Bar Cross tipplers behind me when I'm on personal business," he declared a bit thickly.

There was a laugh at this, but it was a laugh of the slap-on-the-back variety. The Bar Cross men were not going to antagonize the son of Frank Graham, owner of the ranch, and their old man, not by a long shot.

"We're with you, anyway," said one of the men agreeably.

Claude Graham was mollified. Tipping his hat at a rakish angle, he started through the throng in the direction of the dance hall. A hand was laid on his shoulder.

"Where you goin', son?" came a deep voice gruffly.

The youth whirled. "None of your business, Trope," he said hotly. "All you can do for me is to tell this locoed bunch to lay off me, see?"

"I said, where are you goin'?" The tone was harsh now, and the big man who spoke gazed sternly out of small, brownish-green eyes from beneath bushy, red brows that seemed set in a perpetual frown.

The boy's aggressiveness wavered. "Oh, all right, Trope. I suppose you've got to act as my guardian so long's Dad isn't here." His sneer died on his thin lips. "I'm going over to dance with the queen of the Triangle," he declared belligerently. "Got any objections?"

"No . . . sure not," said Trope, turning away. "Go ahead."

Claude Graham continued toward the dance hall almost unnoticed, for most of the members of the crowd looked after the big man—a bulky, bullish figure that plunged straight ahead toward the swinging doors of the Rodeo. Most of the Bar Cross cowpunchers followed him.

"Keeps track of the kid, doesn't he?" spoke a jovial spirit in the throng.

"Old Graham's orders, of course," said another. "Graham thinks a lot of that youngster. Wonder he wouldn't tell Trope to keep him out of the Rodeo. Be better for him."

The crowd thinned, but many followed to the open doors of the dance hall to see whether Claude Graham would have the nerve to carry out his purpose to dance with Connie Cameron.

There was a group about the doors inside the hall, but Claude pushed his way through and stood for a few minutes, blinking in the glare of the many lights before the reflectors along the sides of the big room. A dance was in progress, and he watched the moving couples until finally he glimpsed a face beneath a wealth of gold-spun hair. His eyes burned, and he shifted on his feet. When the dance was over, he hurried a bit unsteadily to where Connie Cameron sat down on a bench on the right side of the hall, admirers flocking to ask for a dance.

The girl's face was a bit flushed from the exercise; her eyes glowed and sparkled with youthful excitement. It was plain that she was happy.

Dances were not frequent in Ransford. It was a big range— all cattle—and the men could not be spared from their work. Only after the fall roundup and the beef cattle were shipped and the hands paid off did everyone join in a general period of festivity—the rodeo. So Connie and the other girls of the Blue Dome range welcomed these few opportunities for meeting each other and enjoying themselves in town.

But Connie Cameron's look of joy faded as Claude Graham came up with an arrogant swagger and, bowing low, addressed her in a tone of excessive familiarity.

"Good evening, Miss Cameron," he said with a rising inflection in his voice.

"Good evening, Mister Graham," she replied agreeably. She had met him two or three times before, and as he was the son of a rancher who was their nearest neighbor on the south— although thirty miles away—she could not be other than polite.

"I'm only staying a . . . a minute, Miss Cameron," he said

with a smile, his eyes glowing brightly. "I've got time for only . . . only one dance. Can I dance this with you?"

The others had drawn back when Claude had arrived, partly because he was something of a bully among the young fellows, and partly because he was the son of an influential rancher. Connie noticed this, and it annoyed her, although she did not know why. Still there was no reason why she should not dance with him—unless it was just because she didn't like him to any extent. She looked around rather helplessly. The music started, and he leaned over and touched her arm.

"Come on, Miss Cameron, be charitable."

She rose. "Do you ask for charity?" she said coolly.

"Aw, be a good sport, Connie, we both live in the same country," he said, putting his arm about her.

She drew back quickly, her eyes darkening. "I hardly think you know me well enough to call me by my first name," she said with a lift of her brows.

"Oh, if you want to stand on ceremony, Miss Cameron. . . ." He paused as he saw the look in her eyes.

"You've been drinking, Mister Graham," she accused.

He grinned. "Jus' a little," he babbled. "It's the spirit of the day, isn't it? Everybody's ta-taking a few on Decoration Day."

"None of the young men I've danced with has been drinking," she said coldly. "Anyway," she added, relenting ever so little, "you're too young to do such a thing."

"Oh, I'm not exactly a yearling," he boasted. "Ain't it a matter of opinion . . . what you said?"

"It's my opinion, Mister Graham," she said firmly. "I'm afraid I cannot dance with you."

"But you promised," he said sharply, his eyes snapping red.

"I didn't know then what I know now," she returned. "I shall have to refuse." She started back to the bench, and he followed.

"Listen," he began, "I. . . ."

He didn't finish the sentence. A strong hand gripped his arm and turned him around. The same hand and arm drew him rapidly toward the door. Then he began to struggle.

"Get away from me, Robbins!" he cried. "Just because you're foreman of the Triangle. . . . Oh, I see. This is a frame-up, eh?"

"It isn't any frame-up so far's I'm concerned," said Robbins. "You were annoying Miss Cameron, and I came to her aid. She'd dance with you all right if you wasn't a little under the weather. You haven't any business in here."

Claude swung with his free hand, but Robbins blocked the blow. Then they were at the door, and the Triangle foreman pushed the youth outside. There was a rush behind them. Robbins turned just in time to step aside to avoid a powerful blow from a man he recognized as a Bar Cross cowpuncher.

He sent the man spinning to the ground with a straight left.

"Bar Cross . . . yo ho . . . Bar Cross!" It was Claude, shouting the signal to his clan.

In a few moments Robbins was fighting for his life. Bar Cross and Triangle men came on the run—the latter suspecting that the call might in some way concern a Triangle man. A crowd came pouring out of the dance hall, those behind pushing those in front until Robbins and his aggressor were forced back and apart. Bar Cross and Triangle men were mingled with those of other outfits.

"Get that Triangle foreman!" shrilled Claude wildly. He had temporarily lost his reason.

The words had the effect of acquainting the members of the two outfits that the trouble was between their men. A mêlée followed, and a free-for-all fight threatened to break instantly. Then a voice was heard roaring an order.

"Bar Cross out in the street. Get together!"

A bulky man, standing on the farther side of the street, with his hand on his gun, had given the command.

Instantly the Bar Cross men began to fight their way out and ran to join him. Members of other outfits not concerned, and other spectators caught in the whirlwind of action, broke away. The Triangle contingent was left standing before the dance hall. Above them in the doorway appeared the white face of Connie Cameron, pressing her hands against her cheeks.

"Oh! Oh!" she cried fearfully. "Come inside, Triangle!"

But the big man had stepped out and was confronting the girl's protectors.

"You, Robbins, what's the big idea?" he demanded harshly.

The Triangle foreman took a step toward him. "Young Graham's carrying his celebration too far, Trope, and you know it," he answered steadily.

"Oh, that's it, is it? Well, what you goin' to do about it?"

"We're not going to permit Miss Cameron to be molested, if that's what you mean," replied Robbins sharply.

Flying hoofs bore down upon them in a cloud of dust before Trope could say anything further. The rider flung himself from the saddle and stepped between them. A gleam of silver shot from beneath his coat in the yellow beams of lamplight.

"None of this, Trope, I won't have it, hear me?" he said loudly, speaking to the Bar Cross foreman. "This isn't open range . . . this is a town. This is the county seat, and I'm the foreman here. I'm the sheriff, Trope, and if you start anything here at this celebration, I'll get you behind the bars for it if it's the last thing I do."

Trope's eyes shot fire, and his lips froze. Then he slowly drew his hand away from his gun. A sneer appeared upon his thick lips.

"All right, Mister Strang," he said in an insulting drawl. "As you say, you're foreman here. Go on with your little party."

"And you keep your bunch inside or take 'em out of town," snapped Strang. "If you don't, I'll deputize every other man in this town and see that you do it!"

Trope's eyes blazed. His hand wavered. But he knew the sheriff had the authority to do just what he threatened to do, and that he would do that very thing. The Bar Cross had the Triangle men outnumbered two to one, but with all the others against them. . . .

He turned sharply on his heel and motioned to his men to disperse.

But Connie Cameron, from her point of vantage, caught the look he threw at the sheriff as the latter turned to his horse.

CHAPTER SIXTEEN

As the Triangle started to move away, Connie called to Robbins, the foreman. He joined her at the top of the steps.

"Tell the men to get the horses," she said quickly, "and then come inside and see me. I will be in the corner to the right of the door, waiting for you."

Robbins turned back to carry out the order, and in a few minutes he returned to find Connie waiting for him.

"I want to thank you, Robbins," she said breathlessly. "Claude Graham was annoying me. I . . . I can't see why he wanted to do it. He had been drinking, and. . . ."

"It's Trope's work," Robbins interrupted in a low tone. "I believe Trope had him milling around in the Rodeo on purpose an' egged him on. He wanted to pick a fight with us. He's always wanting to pick a fight with somebody. He's a gunman, and he knows he's got any of our boys stopped." The foreman's voice was worried.

"That's what I was afraid of, Robbins," Connie agreed. "But I want you to promise me something and get the others of our men to promise. Please do not say anything of what happened here tonight at the ranch to Father . . . to anyone."

"But your father is certain to hear of it sooner or later," said Robbins, surprised.

"Perhaps," the girl agreed. "But not before he comes to town again, and that may be some time. If he should meet any of the Bar Cross men on the south range, I am sure none of them would say anything. Will you please promise, Robbins? I am afraid Father might start trouble."

"I won't say a word and none of the men'll say a word," Robbins promised. "I reckon it wasn't all the kid's fault, although everybody knows he's mean . . . like his father in some ways."

"And now, Robbins, I think we'd better get started," the girl advised. "Perhaps if we go out by way of the cottonwoods behind the barn, we can leave town unobserved by any of the Bar Cross men. I am so afraid that some of the men will meet and get into a fight, and that would mean guns, and. . . ."

She looked at him fearfully.

"And something worse," Robbins supplied grimly. "I can't just see why the Bar Cross should want to pick on us. Claude's mistake wasn't so terrible, after all. I can't get it out of my mind that it was Trope who put it in Claude's head to come over here and annoy you. There's something behind it. Maybe you better stay in town . . . at the hotel . . . and we'll beat it."

Connie drew herself up proudly. "You think they might follow us? And do you think I'm afraid to take my chances with our Triangle men?"

Robbins flushed. "It isn't that, Miss Connie. They might start shooting at us or something. . . ."

"Come. We'll go out the rear of the hall and down to the horses. Then I'll go around into the hotel, get my coat, and be ready to start."

The foreman followed meekly, but with a gleam of admiration in his eyes. He loved Connie Cameron, as did every man on the ranch. She was a real Cameron, through and through, and she had been an able mistress of the great Triangle since the death of her mother some years before.

They passed out one of the rear entrances of the hall almost unobserved, as there was a dance in progress. Then they made their way behind the buildings to the barn, where the Triangle men had congregated. Connie went to the hotel and got her coat, and in a few minutes they were off, riding through the cottonwoods to the stream that flowed through the town, fording the stream, and thence to the road that ran southwestward across the far-flung plain toward the Triangle.

Whether or not they had gotten away unobserved, they were not followed, and after a three-hour spell in the saddle they arrived on the bench above the bottoms where the Triangle ranch buildings were grouped in the shelter of the cliffs above the river, with graceful stands of cottonwoods.

It was about 3:00 in the morning, and, when they rode into the courtyard between the ranch house, bunkhouse, barn, and other buildings, the cowpunchers dismounted at the corrals, and Robbins rode to the front of the house with Connie, to take her horse. She went to her room at once, but, as she was opening the door, her father came out into the hall, holding a lamp.

"Thought you were going to stay in town until morning," he said in a surprised tone.

"I changed my . . . my mind," said the girl. She hadn't thought of what her father would think. "It was a fine night to ride. . . ."

"Connie," he said sternly, "you know they dance about all night at those affairs, and you always stay." He looked at her searchingly.

"I didn't stay tonight, Father, because the . . . the crowd didn't suit me. Now . . . I'm tired."

"Well, go to bed," said Will Cameron doubtfully. "But if there was anything wrong, Robbins will tell me."

Connie crept into bed, thankful that he had not persisted in questioning her. She knew Robbins would know how to explain without involving her and Claude Graham. If her father knew what had happened, he would start straight for the Bar Cross in the south, and that would mean certain trouble.

The first thing she heard when she woke, some four hours afterward, was her father's voice in the courtyard below her window.

"We'll do no such thing!" Will Cameron thundered. "Our cattle stay where they are, and you put in another thousand head today, Robbins. You hear me?"

She looked out her window and saw her father and Robbins in the courtyard. Then she dressed hurriedly and went downstairs. The housekeeper told her that her father had waited to eat breakfast with her, and at that moment Will Cameron came in.

He looked at his daughter keenly, but his face soon lit with a smile of pleasure.

"You look fresh as a daisy, Connie," he told her. "Now for some breakfast, and you'll just naturally be tip-top."

"Daddy, what were you telling Robbins about the cattle," she asked anxiously when he had served her. "Are you going to send more cattle south of the river?"

"I shore am," said the stockman heartily, "and then some. One of Graham's men down there had the nerve to tell Robbins we were getting too far south."

"But, Father, we never have ranged our stock south of the river, and you know Graham doesn't like it."

"And he's never ranged his stock as far north as Rattle Butte, has he?" flared her father. "I told his men we wouldn't go south of Rattle Butte. That's ten miles from the river, and leaves him twenty miles from the butte to his place that he's never used at all, what with his range along the Missouri down there."

The girl looked worried. Her woman's instinct for scenting trouble was uppermost. She knew Claude Graham would exaggerate the incident of the night before at the dance. He would likely tell his father that she had refused to speak to him, or some such thing, and Trope would doubtless back him up.

"It's Trope that I'm thinking of, Father," she finally confessed. "I'm afraid he wants trouble, and. . . ."

"Trope!" blurted Cameron, putting down his knife and fork. "Don't mention his name to me." He scowled and thought for a few minutes. "Foreman of the Bar Cross," he snorted. "That isn't what Graham brought him up here for by a long shot. He's a bully, a gunfighter, and a killer. I reckon Graham figured he'd intimidate me through Trope because I haven't any gunmen. Well, I've lived a long time in this country without gunmen in my outfit, and I guess I can make out still. I thought the trouble would be over when Lennister broke up the Blodgett gang of rustlers and got Blodgett. . . ." He paused, and their eyes met.

Both were thinking of the same thing—of Lennister, the youthful-appearing, gray-eyed, soft-spoken man of uncertain age, whose reputation carried fear into the hearts of men, whose lightning draw was proverbial, whose gun was presumed to be for hire.

"Besides, we need that range down there," Will Cameron resumed, changing the subject and avoiding her eyes. "Our north range is in bad shape. I've got to put the beeves down there. I'm putting them there, and there they're going to stay."

His note of finality convinced the girl that it would be futile to say anything further, so she dropped the subject and did her best to cheer her father as she had always done since the death of her mother.

They had just finished eating when the housekeeper came to the door and announced that Robbins wished to see Cameron. Connie went to the rear door in time to overhear what the foreman said.

"They're down there, Will. Graham an' Trope an' a couple of their men. They say they want to talk to you."

"No wonder they wouldn't come up to the house," said Cameron angrily. "I know what they want, and I know what they're going to get. Send my horse out. I'll go down."

Connie ran out and threw her arms about her father's neck. "Daddy, be careful," she pleaded. "You know what Trope is, as you said, and Graham himself hasn't any too good a reputation."

"I know what shorthorn beeves are going to be worth this fall, and what notes I've got to meet at the bank, and that the Teton Stockman's Association drew the Blue Dome range south limit straight east and west just below Rattle Butte. Connie, go inside. Your old dad is still running the Triangle."

She watched him ride away, and then ran to little Joe Curley, the barn man. "Get my horse, Joe. I'm going for a ride."

Joe hurried to comply. It was the usual thing for the Triangle mistress to go for a ride every morning.

But Connie was not thinking of her usual morning exercise on her beautiful black Spot. Her woman's instinct had become more than a premonition. She faced the truth. Trouble had come to the Triangle.

CHAPTER SEVENTEEN

Will Cameron rode with Robbins south from the buildings to the ford of the river, where they crossed the stream, passed through a grove of cottonwoods, and came out upon a plain that stretched southward to the blue rim of the horizon—unbroken save for the block of purple in the middle distance, which was Rattle Butte.

Four men were sitting their horses, awaiting them. Cameron picked them out as he approached: Frank Graham, tall and rather lanky, but big-boned, with a grayish complexion that neither tanned nor sunburned, close-clipped sandy mustache, and cold, blue eyes that at times seemed colorless. At his side was Trope, his foreman and reputed gunman, hard of face, bulky, glowering, with near-set, small eyes of brownish green. Behind them were two men who evidently were Bar Cross cowpunchers.

"You wouldn't come up to the house," growled Cameron in greeting. "You've never been there yet, Graham."

"I hardly think this is the time to take advantage of your hospitality," said the Bar Cross owner coldly. "I come here. . . ."

"Oh, I know," Cameron broke in. "We might just as well get right down to business, Graham. You're sore because I'm grazing beeves down here. But I sent word to you that I didn't intend to range south of Rattle Butte."

"That isn't the point," snapped Graham. "Your cattle have no business south of the river. I'm going to use this range myself."

Cameron's brows lifted in surprise. "You want this grass up here?" he asked. "What's the matter with all the range you've got south of Rattle? What's the matter with the range south of your home ranch? There's good grass down there, and water."

"I'm buying more cattle," replied Graham stiffly. He had more of the manner of a man of the towns than of the ranges. As Cameron looked at him speculatively, he recalled that Graham had been in the country only six or seven years; none knew very much about him, none had been intimate with him.

"Well, Graham," said the Triangle owner slowly, "I've lived in the Blue Dome country for more than thirty years, and no owner of the Bar Cross has ever had to range cattle north of Rattle Butte. They've been owners, Graham, that have had more stock than you're running," he finished pointedly.

"That has nothing to do with it," said Graham, frowning coldly. "What has been done, and what I do, are two different things." There was a short, harsh laugh at this, and Cameron looked at Trope for the first time, to see a sneer on the man's thick lips. "As far as I can learn, you've never used this range down here, Mister Cameron," Graham continued, too polite to be sincere in his manner. "I believe you are supposed to stick to Blue Dome, and not come south of the river."

"Oh, you suppose that, do you?" cried Cameron, losing his temper. "You've been here a few years and then take it on yourself to make the range limits? Well, Graham, I'm president of the Teton Stockmen's Association, and I know what I'm talking about. The association put the south limit of Blue Dome range just below Rattle Butte twenty years ago! You figure you can get around that?"

Graham smiled wryly. "As president of the association you will probably recall that I am not a member. You doubtless know who belongs," he added sarcastically.

In that instant Cameron suspected a quality of bitterness in the other's voice. Did Graham resent the fact that he had not been asked to join the organization?

"You're pretty far south to belong to our outfit," Cameron observed.

"I'm south of the river, yes," said Graham quickly. "That's just the point. You have no members south of the river. Yet you want to claim this range down here."

"Only a small part of it," said Cameron calmly. "Just from here to Rattle Butte, that's all. There's plenty left to range more stock than you've got, Graham. If you want to put in an application to our. . . ."

"Not by any means," snapped Graham. "I just came up here to tell you that I have a couple thousand head just south of the butte, and I'm sending them north of the butte this morning . . . in charge of Trope, my foreman."

Cameron now looked from one to the other with a light of understanding in his eyes. Then his brows lowered and his face became stern.

"That's an out-and-out threat, Graham," he said evenly. "You're trying to intimidate me with your . . . your confounded gunman."

"Don't say that!" exclaimed Graham sharply. "I'm well within my rights. This is open range. I have no understanding with your association. Trope is my foreman, don't forget that. From this minute he is in charge of my stock on the Rattle Butte range. That's all this morning, Mister Cameron."

Without giving the Triangle owner a chance to reply, he whirled his horse, drove in his steel, and galloped away, followed by the two cowpunchers. Trope lingered, turning his horse leisurely.

"I reckon your cattle are too far south, Cameron!" he called insolently. "I'll need that range, understand? Better think it over and think it over *today*. I haven't any time to monkey around with you even if you are the great high lord of Blue Dome!"

With that and a jarring laugh, he rode away, keeping an eye on the Triangle owner, who seemed on the point of dashing after him.

"How far south are our cattle?" Cameron asked Robbins.

"About six miles," Robbins replied.

"Go down there and keep your eye out," Cameron ordered. "I'm going up on the north range and send down every man that can be spared."

As he rode through the ford, Connie Cameron crept back from her place of concealment at the edge of the trees and mounted. Her face was white, for her fears had proved well founded. The Triangle and Bar Cross were threatened by the ominous specter that ever overshadows open cattle country—a range war.

Will Cameron went north, and that afternoon Triangle men began arriving at the home ranch and crossing the river to the south range. Meanwhile, a man arrived at the ranch with a message from Robbins.

"What is it?" Connie demanded imperatively as the man was changing horses, preparatory to continuing his ride north to see the Triangle's owner.

"Bar Cross cattle north of Rattle Butte," said the man succinctly. "Robbins has driven our herd back this way to keep out of trouble an' keep 'em from mixing with Graham's stock."

Connie stamped her foot in indignation and helplessness. It had come, and she was powerless to prevent it. If only. . . . As she walked toward the house her eyes were wistful. That scoundrel Trope! Of course, in sending him north with the Bar Cross cattle, Graham could conveniently excuse himself from responsibility for anything that might happen. Was all this trouble just because of the range? Connie knew better, and bit her lip. Could she have avoided it by dancing with Claude Graham? The thought disturbed her. After all, was she responsible? If only they had a man who could stand up to Trope.

Will Cameron came in a great hurry late in the afternoon. Without stopping to eat, he changed horses and galloped through the ford and down to the south range. The cattle had been moved north a considerable distance, and the Bar Cross cattle were not a mile south of the Triangle herd. They were still moving north.

Cameron gave orders to shift the Triangle herd to the east, out of the path of the Bar Cross stock. But at sunset the Triangle herd was within two miles of the big bend in the river to the east, where it turned southeast toward the badlands. The cook wagon was put near the river across from the ranch house to be handy to water. Both outfits ceased operations before nightfall, and Cameron rode to the house, his face a study of grim and terrible concentration over the problem presented by Trope's bold move.

"He figures to merge the herds," he muttered absently at the supper table. "But I don't quite get his game in doing it."

"Father," said Connie in sudden inspiration, "why not appeal to Sheriff Strang?"

The eager look in her eyes died as she saw her father sit up and stare at her sternly.

"I've ranched over thirty years in here without asking any help of a sheriff," was all he said.

Even Connie could see that the sheriff would be powerless to regulate range conditions.

"But the association!" she exclaimed. "You're president. . . ."

"That's the trouble," grumbled Cameron. "That's why I don't figure I can go to them. And they're busy."

Will Cameron went into his little office in the front of the house after supper. Connie saw him when he came out, and her hands flew to her breast as she uttered a little cry. She had not seen her father wearing his gun since he had gone with Lennister to get Blodgett.

He came back to the house late that night, and went directly to his room. Connie tried to sleep, but found it impossible. At last she rose, and, putting on her slippers and dressing gown, she went out on the little balcony above the front porch.

It was one of those sublime nights that mark the merging of the prairie spring with summer. The purple canopy of the sky was hung with clusters of gleaming stars. The trembling leaves of the cottonwoods were silver spangles against the shadow of the bluffs. The purring lullaby of the river sounded faintly above the plaintive rustle of the wind in cottonwood and alder and quaking aspen. The cool air was laden with the scent of lilacs and the breath of the fields in the bottoms.

It was a scene of indescribable peace—soothing to the senses. So Connie thought. How she loved this ranch home where she had been born, where she had always lived save for the three years at school in a prairie city far to southward.

Her thoughts were rudely interrupted by sudden sounds that were not of the elements—echoes, muffled, then clear-cut as the wind changed momentarily. Sharp reports came from beyond the dark line of trees along the river below the fields. A short silence and then they came again—the unmistakable reports of guns.

For a few moments Connie clutched the rail of the balcony to steady herself. Then the faintness passed and she flew into the hall. But there was no need to rouse her father. She saw his light shining through the keyhole and crack of his door, heard him moving about hurriedly. In another moment he flung open the door and ran past her, fully dressed and armed. She sensed vaguely that he had kept his clothes on. She moved down the hall as the housekeeper came out of her room, just in time to steady her as she groped faintly.

Joe Curley, the barn man, was already up and out when Will Cameron reached the courtyard. In less than three minutes Cameron was in the saddle, galloping for the ford. Through the shadowy, interlaced branches of the trees he saw a red glare, and, as he crossed the stream and burst through the trees to the plain, he saw the cook wagon in flames.

Flying hoofs echoed to the left, and he turned in that direction. He saw darting shadows, then spurts of flame, and the air rang with the barking of guns. To the right was a dark mass— the cattle. A rider bore down upon him from that direction, and red flashes streamed from a gun. Cameron fired twice and saw the oncoming horse rear as its rider slumped in the saddle, fell, and came clear, to lie motionlessly on the plain.

Just ahead he heard Robbins's voice shouting a command: "Take to the trees!"

The Triangle men evidently were to the left, close to the river. Cameron turned his horse toward them. He saw horsemen on the right bearing in that direction, and suddenly one spurted toward him—a huge form in the saddle on a big horse.

He jerked his gun out again and swung it up as they came together. A ball of fire seemed to burst in his face, and a hot brand seared his brain. He was conscious of falling, of striking something, then came darkness, total darkness, as sudden as the blowing out of a match.

Robbins brought the still, limp form of Will Cameron to the ranch. He carried his unconscious employer upstairs to his room, with Connie, her face white as death, following, trailed by the housekeeper. They washed the wound in Cameron's head, dressed it, and then Robbins took off his clothes and put him in bed. The girl and the housekeeper came in to nurse him and watch over him while Robbins hurried to call a man and send him at breakneck speed to Ransford for the doctor.

When Robbins returned, he stood uncertainly in the doorway, looking at the two women and the still form in the bed. "I'm going back south of the river," he told Connie in a low voice. "They've gone south again now. They won't be back tonight after . . . after this."

Connie nodded dully. There seemed to be a film over her eyes, as if the tragic events of the night had stunned her.

"I'll go make you some strong coffee, dearie, since you won't try to get some rest," said the housekeeper.

Connie looked at her with a blank expression as she left the room.

Will Cameron began to mutter in delirium. "I . . . see . . . you. I see . . . you. . . ."

As he whispered the name, Connie seemed to come to herself with the suddenness of an electric shock. She straightened, and her eyes flashed. Her lips no longer trembled, but froze into a fine, white line. She stepped to her father's table, opened the ink bottle there, and wrote hurriedly on a sheet of paper. Then she sealed the note in an envelope and addressed it. Her face and eyes appeared years older as she walked to the head of the stairs and called in a queer voice to the housekeeper.

"Call Joe Curley," she instructed. "Send him here to me, at once."

Joe came, his face white and his eyes startled, and stood before her with his hat held nervously in his hands.

"Ride to Conroy, Joe," said the girl, handing him the envelope. "Ride to Conroy, and deliver that. If he isn't there, find him. Don't come back until you've delivered that message . . . understand?"

The little wrangler's eyes popped as he read the name on the envelope. Then he thrust it inside his shirt, and his jaw clicked shut.

"I'll deliver it, Miss Connie," he said simply, but in deadly earnest.

"Take Spot," she ordered. "He's fast."

The housekeeper came with the coffee, and Connie sipped it, her eyes gleaming with determination. The housekeeper marveled at the change in her, and hesitated to speak.

Robbins came again in two hours, just before dawn, with the information that the herds were merged, and that two of the men had been wounded, and that he had put them in the bunkhouse.

The girl looked up at him keenly. "Do you know who shot Father?" she asked quietly.

"I . . . couldn't say for sure," replied the Triangle foreman. "But I have my opinion."

"Yes, yes, I know," said the girl half to herself. "We know, of course. We both know. Robbins, I've sent for a man to take charge. This isn't father's kind of a game, it isn't yours, and it isn't mine. It takes a certain kind of a man to play this kind of a game. I've sent for him."

Robbins's look was puzzled. He, too, noticed the grim change in the girl as she sat by the bedside holding her father's hand.

"Who've you sent for, Miss Connie?"

"I've sent for a man who will know what to do," she said fiercely. "Robbins, I've sent for Lennister."

CHAPTER EIGHTEEN

At 10:00 A.M. Dr. French arrived from Ransford. He found Will Cameron still unconscious, delirious with fever, and watched over by Connie, who looked pale and wan, but whose brave spirit was undaunted. After an examination he announced that he would have to remove the bullet that had lodged in the stockman's skull, and ordered Connie from the room. The housekeeper was recruited to assist him.

Connie went out on the porch, and it was there that Robbins found her when he returned to the ranch for the second time with an amazing piece of information.

"The Bar Cross men are driving the whole herd south," he told her. "They outnumber our men two to one, and I don't know how to stop them without bringing on a fight, and we wouldn't have a show." His air was gloomy. "But we're ready to try," he added grimly, looking to the mistress of the Triangle for assent.

"You mean they are driving *our* cattle south with theirs?" asked the girl in bewilderment.

"That's the size of it, Miss Connie. They've got about fifteen hundred head of their own, and they're mixed with a thousand or twelve hundred wearing our iron. If you say the word. . . ."

But Connie shook her head. "Is Trope in charge?" she asked absently, thinking deeply.

"No, Trope hasn't showed up this morning," replied Robbins with a puzzled frown. "That beats me."

"Get my horse, Robbins," she ordered. "I'll take a look."

She quickly donned her riding clothes and, after receiving the assurance of the housekeeper that her father was not liable to succumb to the operation of removing the bullet, rode away with Robbins. One look at the edge of the plain south of the river was enough. The big herd was already a mere blot under a cloud of dust some distance in the south.

"I'd have told you the minute they started, Miss Connie, but I tried to argue and trick 'em out of it," explained Robbins. "I don't see how we're going to stop 'em unless we raid 'em with every man on the ranch, and then we'd have a running fight on our hands." The foreman was visibly excited and at a loss.

"You're right," she said. "We can't stop them at present." After all, Robbins had always depended upon Will Cameron. The stockman had repeatedly told him not to make a move without his consent. In fact, Robbins had been a sort of figurehead, for Cameron had been the real foreman-manager of the Triangle as well as the owner.

Suddenly the girl brightened. "Robbins," she remarked, "don't you see what they're doing? They're stealing our cattle! Let them drive them away. We'll make that old Graham pay for this."

He caught her meaning instantly. "Dog-gone, Miss Connie, but I believe you're right. What'll I do with the men? Keep 'em here at the bunkhouse . . . bring 'em in, I mean? The cook wagon's burned, and all they've had today is coffee."

"Yes, bring them in for the present," the girl directed.

"And will you have the doctor go in and look at those two men in the bunkhouse, Miss Connie? They're both shot, but not bad."

"I forgot all about them," said Connie in self-reproach. "I'll look in myself and send the doctor in as soon . . . as soon as he can go. You've had breakfast? Good. Keep your eye on what takes place down here, Robbins, and report to me."

They had been riding south at a trot, and now Connie stopped. After a long look across the plain toward the moving herd and the big, square outline of Rattle Butte, she turned her horse and started back for the house.

Trope had doubtless gone down to the Bar Cross to report. She pressed her lips firmly together, and her eyes flashed. Then she lifted her head and seemed to shake a weight from her shoulders. Joe Curley had ridden away on Spot—her horse—one of the fastest horses on the Triangle. He must be close to the town of Conroy by this time—perhaps there already. She felt a thrill. What was it Lennister had told her that evening he had left the ranch? *If ever you need me . . . send for me?* He had meant it, too. And she had called him a paid killer. Now she was waiting for him, hoping for him, longing for him with all her heart. Why? To buy his services. Yes, she might as well acknowledge it to herself. And why not? Hadn't Trope shot her father down in cold blood? She had heard Will Cameron whisper Trope's name in his delirium. Wasn't he a notorious gunfighter—a killer? Wasn't she entitled to protect the Triangle now that her father was unable to take charge? But then, Lennister knew cows, she reflected. He would accept the temporary management of the ranch under the circumstances. That was why she was sending for him, she thought with a sigh of relief. To take charge in the emergency.

She had crossed the river, but was still in the trees below the bottoms, when a rider came suddenly into the trail ahead of her and drew rein. Connie's face went white when she recognized him. It was Claude Graham.

He took off his hat as she rode up, and a peculiar expression on his face caused her to look at him sharply. Before she could ride around him, or order him out of the way, he spoke contritely.

"Good morning, Miss Cameron. I'm sorry for what happened the other night in town."

Connie was taken by surprise. It hadn't occurred to her that he would take occasion to apologize to her. Moreover, he appeared to be in earnest.

"Are you sure that you mean that?" she returned coldly.

"Yes, I do. I came up here to see if I couldn't do something for you."

Connie now was actually astonished. But instantly she was reminded of what had taken place since that night, of her feeling of responsibility for it. After all, Claude Graham had started it.

"I don't wish you to do anything for me," she said haughtily. "Please draw your horse aside, Mister Graham."

"But, Miss Cameron, hear me out," he persisted. "I know you're in trouble, and if you want me to, I'll see if I can get Dad to lay off."

She looked at him in horrified understanding, although he misconstrued her attitude. He was making a proposition to bring about peace? So then he did know what the trouble was all about. It was more than a mere difficulty over the range.

"I'll tell him to lay off if you want me to, Miss Cameron," Claude was saying for the second time.

Connie's face went red, then white. She drove in her spurs, and her mount lunged against his. As his horse reared back, she rose in her stirrups and struck at him with her quirt. The leather landed on his shoulder, and then she was galloping for the house.

Her face was still burning with indignation when she went inside. Dr. French was eating a lunch in the kitchen. He nodded cheerfully.

"Came out all right," he said briskly. "He'll pull through, but he probably won't recover consciousness for a day or two. Not till the fever's spent. No getting about for him for a month at least, I'd say. I'll stay here tonight. Why, child . . . help her, madam."

The reaction had finally claimed the girl, and she sank back into the housekeeper's arms in a faint.

"We'll put her to bed," the doctor decided, his professional instincts awakened immediately as he ministered to her.

When Connie opened her eyes, she was in bed. She drank a potion the doctor gave her and immediately fell asleep.

After a time—a long time, it seemed—voices came to her as from a great distance. She did not open her eyes, but she knew that she was awake, and she listened. The voices came from the courtyard.

"I tell you, you can't disturb her . . . and that's final!" It was the sharp, barking voice of Dr. French.

Connie moved, opened her eyes, and sat up. She felt refreshed, repossessed of her strength. She rose and went to the window. In the courtyard, sitting their horses, were Sheriff Strang and Trope. As she looked, they dismounted.

She flew to put on her clothes, and in the space of a few minutes she was dressed and hurrying down the stairs. The sheriff, Trope, and the doctor had come around to the front of the house, and Connie stepped out on the porch and looked down at them coldly.

Sheriff Strang removed his hat. "Howdy, Miss Cameron," he greeted. He seemed uncomfortable, and scowled at Trope, who looked up at her curiously, lazily, almost insolently.

"Your father is better, I hear," the sheriff continued, "and I'm sure glad of it."

"Did you come here to tell me that?" she asked with a lift of her brows.

"Well, not exactly," he confessed uneasily. "You see . . . er . . . well, Miss Cameron, the Bar Cross has made a complaint against your father and the Triangle men. They say your men attacked them and shot two of their men, and. . . ."

"Sheriff Strang, you've known my father a great many years," said the girl scornfully, "and you know that could not be true. My father was shot from his saddle, and two of our men wounded when . . . it was that . . . that *beast* who shot him!"

She pointed at Trope, but the Bar Cross foreman merely flicked the ash from his cigarette nonchalantly.

"Then . . . if you can prove it, Miss Cameron . . . you will have to make complaint, also," said Strang, more nervous than ever. "But I have to serve a warrant when one is sworn out. That's my duty. I have a warrant for your . . . your father, Miss Cameron, and I'll have to serve it as soon as he is well enough to be seen."

She saw the glimmer of a smile on Trope's lips.

"You think you can do anything like this . . . you murdering beast of a Bar Cross gunfighter? You . . . you. . . ." Her voice died away as the swift pound of hoofs came from the courtyard, and a rider arrived in a cloud of dust.

A little, inarticulate cry came from Connie as the horseman flung himself from his saddle and stood before them.

"Lennister!" she sobbed. Then she sobered, and her eyes darted fire. "You're in charge here, Lennister . . . I hire you this minute. Tell that man to leave the ranch!"

Lennister turned and leisurely inspected Trope, who she had indicated, and who had stepped back with his hand on his gun as he heard the name.

Sheriff Strang's jaw dropped, but he did not seem altogether to disapprove of the situation.

"You heard what she said?" Lennister inquired in a drawl.

"I ain't hard of hearing," snarled Trope. "You've been here before, I take it. Well, you're not chasing me off."

"I reckon you must be the Troop or Trip or Tripe or some

such name that Joe was telling me about on the way down," said Lennister. "Well, Mister Trope, I'll have to tell you to leave the ranch. You heard me get my orders."

"You seem to be glad enough to take 'em from who gave 'em to you," sneered Trope.

Lennister's eyes hardened. "Get out!" he commanded.

Trope's eyes blazed, and his hand tightened on his gun. It was out of its holster a bare two inches when Lennister leaped and caught him on the jaw with a powerful right.

Trope went spinning backward and fell. He twisted and looked up to find Lennister covering him with his gun, glaring at him narrowly.

"You going?" Lennister's words brimmed with warning.

Trope got to his feet; his face was contorted with rage. His eyes were points of flickering fire.

"This takes it out of your hands, Sheriff," he snarled as he backed to his horse.

"Keep that right hand high," commanded Lennister sharply.

Trope's curses floated back to them as he sped away.

Lennister turned to the others. Sheriff Strang was first to speak. "You know I told you, Lennister, after that Blodgett affair, that you couldn't come back into this country as a paid gunman," he said slowly. "I'm still standing by my word."

"He's here to manage the Triangle until father has recovered," said Connie Cameron, facing the sheriff and clenching her palms. "And I am responsible."

"In that case he can stay, Miss Cameron," said the sheriff, bowing gravely.

Chapter Nineteen

Sheriff Strang, Dr. French, Lennister, and Connie ate supper in the Triangle dining room at sunset. The sheriff and doctor talked amiably, the former apparently seeking to avoid the eyes of Connie Cameron. He wasn't altogether sure about his duty in this case, and he wondered in just what capacity Will Cameron's daughter had engaged the services of Lennister. He studied the latter covertly, decided he was about twenty-six years old, good eyes—although he had caught a certain look in them when he had ordered Trope to go that revealed what he thought was another and dangerous side to his character. Yes, Lennister was undoubtedly dangerous. The official stole a glance at Connie and saw that she also was regarding her new foreman surreptitiously. As for Lennister himself, he said little or nothing. Early in the meal he had curbed attempts to engage him in conversation.

After supper the doctor went back to the sick room and the sheriff took his departure.

"You needn't bother much about that . . . that warrant, Miss Cameron," he told the girl with a friendly smile. "As you say, I've known your father a long time, and I don't believe all I hear. It's hard for me to handle troubles such as these . . . these affairs between ranches. But are you sure you can handle your new man?"

"I have every confidence that Lennister will obey my orders," replied the girl. "But, in an emergency like this, I will naturally depend a great deal on his judgment."

"That's what has me worried," said Strang slowly. "That man is as quiet and docile as a kitten, and that's what makes him all the more dangerous."

He approached Lennister, who was sitting on the porch steps, smoking.

"I'm going in to town, Lennister," he announced, "but I want you to remember one thing. I expect you to keep your gun cold."

Lennister gazed at him quizzically. "There are times, Sheriff, when a cold gun means a cold heart," he said enigmatically.

"Meaning a dead one . . . *I* know," the sheriff said, "but I'm giving you a sort of a friendly warning."

"Thanks, Sheriff. Did you give Trope the same warning?"

"I did," said Strang with a scowl. "I meant it even if he is in another county down there."

"That starts us even at the barrier," Lennister drawled.

The sheriff opened his mouth, closed it, scowled, then nodded to Connie and took his departure.

"Will you come in the office, Lennister?" Connie invited.

He rose to his splendid height and removed his hat. She noted his clear-cut profile in the last light of the sunset, his kindling gray eyes as he looked at her suddenly, then instinctively her gaze fell to the butt of the gun on his right thigh, the slim, brown, tapering fingers of that lightning hand above it, hooked in the cartridge belt. It gave her a feeling of security—that hand and that gun. And suddenly she looked up at him, startled. Was *that* why she had sent for him?

"Couldn't we talk out here, ma'am?" he asked. "I admire to look at those lilacs and sniff their perfume. I've had few flowers in my life, Miss Connie."

Something in his voice held her rooted to the spot in sheer wonder. It all seemed so incongruous—this man whose gun was said to be for hire, who had shot outlaws and perhaps others in terrible fashion at the risk of his own life, who laughed at death when matching his draw with killers—this man talking of lilacs and flowers. For several moments she was disconcerted and not sure of herself. But she motioned to him to sit down on the steps, and sat down on the step above him.

"Why did you send for me, ma'am?" he asked dreamily.

"Because the Triangle and Bar Cross have become engaged in a range war," she explained, "because Trope shot my father and he is unable to look after the ranch affairs, because the Bar Cross is playing the kind of a game that neither Robbins nor I understand how to meet. I thought perhaps you . . . I need someone. . . ." She faltered.

"I see," he said slowly, without looking at her. "Are you sure Trope shot your father?"

"He's about the only man on the Bar Cross who would dare do it," said the girl bitterly, "and father keeps mentioning him in his delirium . . . keeps saying he saw him. Robbins believes he was the man. Trope has a terrible reputation."

"I know," admitted Lennister. "Joe was telling me things on the way down. I came as fast as I could after I got your note. Had to hold in my bay a little to keep Joe along, or I'd've been here sooner. What started all the trouble, ma'am?"

The quality of his voice, coolly confident, sympathetic, calm, reassured her, and she explained what had happened at length, omitting nothing from the time they had first driven the cattle south of the river, including both meetings with Claude Graham, and Trope's ultimatum—everything to the time of his coming.

He was silent for a while. "Is it all right for me to smoke, Miss Connie?" he asked.

She laughed softly. "I was born on the Triangle, Lennister," she reminded him.

"You're real Western then," he observed as he took out papers and tobacco and fashioned a cigarette.

The purple twilight fell over the land, and a mockingbird saluted it with a concert. The wind freshened and filled the leaves of the cottonwoods with vague whisperings. One by one the stars began their march across the sky, the bluffs gathered their shadows, and the night shook out its satiny skirts of darkness.

"Yes, I reckon you're real Western, Miss Connie," said Lennister after he had touched the fire to his cigarette. He paused, and then: "Do you want me to kill Trope?"

Connie Cameron drew in her breath quickly. "No, no, no," she insisted in an anxious undertone. "Did you think I sent for you for that?" She placed a hand on his shoulder. "Did you, Lennister?"

"No, I reckon not," he confessed whimsically. "But I'm here for orders."

"Would you go out and deliberately kill Trope if I told you to do it?" she asked, incredulous.

"Yes, I probably would," he answered bluntly.

She drew back. What manner of man was this she had hired? She felt a stab at her heart. She had hoped—but *why* had she hoped? She might have known? What could she expect? Hadn't she seen him kill an outlaw? True, he had to do so or lose his own life, but. . . .

"And then again, I might not," he said suddenly.

Connie breathed freely again. "I'm . . . I'm glad to hear you . . . say that," she stammered.

"I might chase him out of the country," said Lennister as though talking to himself. "Then . . . if he wouldn't go . . . it would be up to him." He looked up at her and she thought she caught a gleam of humor in his eyes, although she could not see them very well.

"I do not want anyone killed," she said severely. "I want you to heed the sheriff's warning and keep your gun cold. That is, unless . . . unless. . . ." She found herself unable to go on.

"I understand, Miss Connie," he said, rising abruptly. "Is your acting foreman . . . what's his name?"

"Robbins."

"Down south of the river tonight?"

"Yes, he's down there keeping watch on what the Bar Cross is doing. But I expect him back any minute."

"Then I'll drop into the bunkhouse until he comes," said Lennister as she rose. "When he comes, I'd like to see him, of course. My horse is pretty tired, I reckon. If I should need one, I suppose there's one handy?"

"The men have their strings in the corrals. Joe Curley will find you one, and I'll tell him to see that you get the best."

"Thanks." He turned to go. "I didn't expect you to say you wanted me to kill Trope, ma'am," he called to her softly, "but I may have to do it."

She stood on the porch, breathless, thrilled, fearful, and watched him disappear around the corner of the house. There was the peace of perfect security in her heart, even though she blamed herself for it.

CHAPTER TWENTY

Several of the men in the bunkhouse nodded to Lennister when he entered, and all looked at him curiously and respectfully. Joe Curley had spread the news of his coming, and already the incident of his clash with Trope was the subject of awed comment.

Lennister chose an empty bunk, hung his hat on a peg, unbuckled his gun belt, and placed it at the head. Then he lay down on the bunk and closed his eyes. Some might have thought he was sleeping, but this was not the case. He was reviewing carefully everything Connie Cameron had told him, weighing each incident and detail in his mind, formulating his plans. And the girl herself occupied no small measure of his thoughts.

It was thus that Robbins found him when he returned to the ranch an hour later. Lennister rose, buckled on his gun, put on his hat, and led the way into the courtyard.

"Miss Connie told me you'd taken charge," Robbins said. "I'm glad you've come, Lennister," he added frankly. "We're up against it with that Bar Cross crowd."

"Where have they got the cattle?" Lennister asked.

"Down near Rattle Butte. I think they have a camp down there."

"I know every foot of that country, almost," mused Lennister. "I was in there when I first came up this way. There's a creek or some springs at the butte, eh, Robbins?"

"Springs and marshy ground below 'em," Robbins replied.

"Trees on both sides of the butte as I remember it?"

"That's right, and the trees run quite a spell southeast of Rattle, too," Robbins affirmed.

"Can you see to it that I get a good horse?" asked Lennister.

"Joe has one for you out of my own string. Why, you going to ride tonight?" Robbins seemed very much surprised.

"I'm going to the Bar Cross, but you needn't say anything about it to Miss Connie," said Lennister. "Listen, Robbins, are the men ready to go?"

"All fit. They've had plenty of rest this afternoon."

"Good. Now, Robbins, you get the men out after a while and slope down southeast so that the Bar Cross bunch with the cattle can't see you. Go a good ways east. It'll be along toward morning before the moon gets up, and you'll be able to slip back to the trees southeast of the butte. Get the trees between you and the Bar Cross camp before you go in. Bring along an extra horse for me. Better let the night hawk trail you with a string for we'll probably need 'em. Keep far enough away from the butte so they can't hear the horses. Get in there by midnight and wait there for me."

"Wait for you," Robbins repeated. "We'll do it. An' if you shouldn't show up . . . then what?"

"Then hotfoot it back to the ranch," said Lennister grimly. "But I've a notion I'll be back before morning."

"They'll probably have a look-out up on the butte," observed Robbins thoughtfully.

"I was thinking of that," said Lennister, "and that's why you'd better hustle down there before long and get in while it's dark . . . before the moon. I'll try and take care of the look-out on the way down. If you can slope out of here without Miss Connie knowing it, so much the better."

"She is sitting up with her father until midnight, when the housekeeper takes her place," Robbins volunteered. "We can go out in pairs by the lower road beyond the barn, I reckon."

"That's good," said Lennister. "No need causing Miss Connie any more worry or starting her to wondering. I'll be going, Robbins."

A few minutes later Lennister was fording the river. He came out of the trees upon the plain and started northeast, riding at a stiff lope. Robbins had seen to it that he had a good mount, and he covered the miles at an excellent rate, keeping far to the east of Rattle Butte where the Bar Cross cowpunchers had taken the big herd.

Lennister had been in the country before, as he had told Robbins. He knew the exact location of the Bar Cross ranch house, which was some ten miles southwest of Rattle Butte on a little stream that flowed from the northwest into the big Missouri in the south. He had, on the occasion when he first came north from the Musselshell country, stopped at the very camp Robbins had spoken of at Rattle Butte. There had been no one there then, and he had spent a night in the cabin on the west side of the butte. He had gone to the top of the butte, too, for a survey of the country, and he was familiar with the big tableland up there that could be reached from one side only—the east.

All this he had in mind when he had given his instructions to Robbins. But first he was going to the Bar Cross—after he had had a look on top of the butte.

As he rode, he took advantage of every shadow, of every piece of cover, of every depression and miniature coulée in the surface of the broad plain. In time he brought up at the line of trees and willows southeast of the butte. Keeping in the shadow of these, he walked his horse to a point just below the butte's eastern slope. This slope furnished the only means of reaching the top of Rattle, for on the other side the butte fell away in sheer precipices to the plain.

For a spell he deliberated. He decided that if a look-out had been posted on top of the butte, he would be on the north side, probably the northwest corner where he could keep watch to the north, in which direction was the Triangle, and to the west where the herd was likely bedded down.

There were scrub growths of buckbrush on either side of the slope, marking its edge. For some time Lennister waited and listened without hearing a sound save the usual vague noises of the night. He surmised it could not be more than 9:00 P.M. Finally he rode boldly up the slope, keeping well to the right, near the buckbrush. He remembered that there was a miniature lake in the center of the tableland on top of the butte formed by the winter snows and spring rains. There were willows about it, and a few trees.

He gained the tableland, rode to the shelter of the trees, pushed through to the western side, and surveyed the flat prospect of level ground that extended to the western and northern edges of the tableland. But no look-out was in sight. Either Trope, if he was with the herd, did not think it necessary to post a look-out, or else he considered it too early.

Lennister rode close to the western edge, dismounted, went forward on foot, and looked below. Just under the butte was the Bar Cross cabin. Light shone from its windows, smoke came from the pipe thrust through its roof, and men were moving about. Beyond the trees nearly surrounding the cabin the big herd of Bar Cross and Triangle cattle had been bedded down.

Lennister watched the dark forms of the men moving about for some time, but could not make out the bulky form of Trope. Finally he returned to his horse, mounted, and retraced his way down the east slope to the line of trees. He rode some distance southeast, and then crossed the little stream, left the cover of the scanty timber behind, and struck due west, riding at a fast gallop.

In half an hour he was avoiding bands of cattle, and in an

hour he rode down a long coulée to the trees along the stream that flowed past the Bar Cross ranch house. Here he found a road and turned upstream, keeping a sharp look-out. He came to a fence and a gate and passed through, with a field on his right that extended to the line of some high bluffs. He was approaching the Bar Cross ranch house.

Here he left the road and sought the shelter of the trees below the fields along the stream. After proceeding a distance of half a mile he saw a light glimmer through the branches of a windbreak of cottonwoods ahead. These trees proved the eastern boundary of the big yard surrounding the house. There were numerous shrubs and a few trees in the yard below the house, and Lennister dismounted among the trees along the stream.

The lights he had seen shone from two windows of a room in the front of the house. One of these windows was on the porch side, and the other was in the side of the house toward Lennister. Two tall shrubs grew on either side of this window, and there were several shrubs between Lennister and the house in the sloping yard.

He tied his horse, hitched his gun, and ran for the shelter of the first shrub. Having gained it, he waited a few moments before continuing to the second shrub, and in this way he reached the shelter of what proved to be two large lilac bushes growing on either side of the window.

There was no stir of life about the house, and after a short period of vigil Lennister removed his hat and peered cautiously in the screened window.

The room was lit by a shaded lamp on the table in the center. Near the table a man was sitting in an armchair, and Lennister at once recognized Frank Graham, owner of the Bar Cross, by the descriptions he had been given of him. There was no one else in the room, and the house was still.

Graham was looking at a paper, held in one hand while he

tapped the arm of his chair with the fingers of his other hand nervously. In the shaded light of the lamp his face looked pasty and the eyes colorless. He was dressed in a business suit, with collar and bow tie, and across his shirt front was a black ribbon. Lennister noted the ribbon and wondered why the ranch owner was not using his eyeglasses. But the ribbon might be attached to a watch. Lennister shrugged. A small matter.

Inspection of the room showed two doors, one at the left, evidently leading into the dining room, and the other near the front, probably and most likely leading into the hall that opened onto the porch. This door interested Lennister. He took careful note of the arrangement of the various articles of furniture in the room and then slipped away from the window to the corner of the porch.

There was no sign of movement anywhere. Lennister rounded the porch and walked to its other end, where he could see the courtyard on the north side of the house. The bunkhouse was on the side, and the barns were almost under the bluffs. But no light showed.

He stepped lightly upon the porch, tiptoed to the screen door, opened it noiselessly, and entered the hall. The door to the room where Graham was sitting was the first on the left as the light shining through the crack indicated.

Lennister grasped the knob, opened the door quickly, and stepped inside as Graham started up in his chair. He looked coolly into the black bore of Lennister's gun as the latter closed the door softly.

Lennister made a gesture of warning and looked closely at the Bar Cross owner.

Graham, after a long stare, motioned to a chair in front of him. "Sit down," he said in a low voice, carrying the hint of a sneer. "I happen to know who you are, Lennister."

CHAPTER TWENTY-ONE

Lennister sat down without showing any surprise over the fact that Graham knew him. He balanced his gun on his knee and surveyed the Bar Cross owner at length while the latter toyed nervously with the thin silk cord on his shirt front.

"You look quite prosperous," said Lennister finally in an undertone, "dressed in those city clothes thataway. Maybe you won't forget to use your society voice while we're talking." He made a significant gesture to emphasize his speech.

"I suppose you're after money," said Graham in a tone of contempt. "I understand you're an alleged reformed bandit making a living by hiring out your gun. But I know better."

"Those are hard words, Graham," Lennister observed mildly.

"I expect they're true. However, I can tell you now that there isn't five hundred dollars on this ranch, but I suppose I'll have to open the safe for you to prove it."

Lennister shook his head slowly. "No, you won't have to do that, Graham. I believe you."

Graham looked puzzled, and he agitated the silk ribbon more than ever. "Then what do you want?" he demanded.

"I want to know what the play is against the Triangle," replied Lennister coolly.

"Oh, you've heard about . . . about our range trouble?"

It was Lennister's turn to be astonished. It was quite evident from Graham's reply and manner of speaking that he had not heard that Lennister had been employed by Connie Cameron.

Trope, then, hadn't been at the home ranch since the trouble at the Triangle, nor had he sent word.

"Yes, I heard about it," he answered. "Sounds serious to me."

Graham leaned toward him and his colorless eyes now sparkled eagerly. "You came here to get hired on?" he asked. "To join up with the outfit?"

"You mean you want to hire my gun?" Lennister countered.

"If you want to put it that way," said Graham with a nod.

Lennister frowned. "Graham, you're just a plain skunk. You're not cow people, and you know it. This is the first ranch you ever owned, and you've got to have a bully and a gunfighter to run it for you. You're just naturally mean and contemptible and low . . . and I can prove it."

The effect of this speech on the Bar Cross owner was to cause him to sit up, tug nervously at the black ribbon, and stare with a look in which uncertainty, fear, and anger were commingled.

"Any man who will threaten and make war against a girl, steal her cattle, and shoot down her father, deserves shooting, Graham," said Lennister in a low, sinister voice. "I've shot men for less."

Graham wet his lips with a dry tongue. "You . . . what have you to do with it?" he managed to get out.

"Miss Cameron hired me this afternoon as foreman of the Triangle until her father recovers and saves you and Trope from being charged with murder."

The Bar Cross owner seemed to bring himself together with a jerk of the shoulders. His expression changed. His eyes were coldly calculating, although his nervousness was visibly increased.

"You come here to threaten me?" he asked.

Lennister's eyes were brimming with contempt. "I wouldn't threaten you but once, Graham, you know that."

Graham's face went a shade whiter. "Then what is it you want?" he asked.

"I just want you to know that I'm on the job for Miss Cameron," said Lennister, leaning forward in his chair so that his gaze locked with the other's. "And I want to give you a little advice . . . don't sneer, I've given advice to better men than you, Graham, and they've taken it . . . and then I want to know if you want to go through with the thing."

"What do you advise?" Graham's tone was more than mildly curious.

"First I'd see that those Triangle cattle are cut out of that herd you have up north. Then I reckon I'd tell Trope to stay south of that butte and out of Ransford. I believe I'd do that sure, Graham. And I'd send that whipper-snapper, no-good, misled son of yours up to Miss Cameron to apologize on his knees, even if she wouldn't accept the apology."

Graham's eyes flashed at Lennister's last words, and Lennister sat back with a look of satisfaction.

"That hurts, eh? Gets you where your skin ain't so tough to know that the daughter of the Triangle ain't breaking her neck to link up, maybe, with the Bar Cross? You kind of went at it the wrong way, importing Trope and all, to make those old-timers up there think you were good enough for 'em, Graham. That might be why you haven't been asked to join the Teton Association. Ever think of that?"

Again Graham's eyes blazed, and once more Lennister knew he had hit home.

"What do I care for their association?" he gritted.

Lennister smiled, but his eyes narrowed. "You're a jealous rat, Graham, besides being a sneaking coyote when it comes to range manners. Listen, when I have a job on my hands, I start by going straight to headquarters. In this case headquarters is right here. I want to know if you want to go through with this thing, understand?"

"I understand," said Graham with an evil smile. "I quite understand that you've hired your gun and lent your black reputation to that girl up there. I'm wondering . . . I'm wondering what your the price is."

"Be careful, Graham!" Lennister's left hand moved in the flash of an eye, and the room echoed to the sharp sound of the slap on the rancher's mouth.

Then Graham's hand jerked at the cord, there was a flash of silver, and the house rang with the shrill notes of the whistle he blew as Lennister leaped upon him.

They went backward over the chair, Lennister's gun flying out of his hand. He grasped Graham about the body, but the rancher wrenched himself free with a display of strength Lennister had not suspected he possessed. Both leaped to their feet, and Lennister recovered his gun as Graham sprang to the table. The next instant the light was out and the room in darkness. Lennister heard a drawer of the table pulled open and jumped to grasp Graham again, anticipating his purpose. A gun blazed almost in his face and he dropped to the floor, his own weapon held ready.

For several seconds there was silence. Then came the sound of someone coming down the stairs. Lennister moved toward the door leading into the dining room. He was in shadow, but as he touched the knob, Graham's gun blazed again, and Lennister heard the bullet splinter the panel near his head. He moved back quickly along the wall to the other door, and as he threw it open, it was also opened by someone on the other side.

"He's at the door!" Graham cried. "Get him there!"

The rancher's gun spoke again, and there was another sharp report as a gun spat fire. Then Lennister's own weapon roared, the dark form in the doorway swung aside, and Lennister plunged through.

A man was coming up the steps, and Lennister brought his

weapon barrel crashing down on the newcomer's head. He ran to the end of the porch and leaped over. Then he sped down the yard, putting such cover as offered between him and the house. The sharp reports of a gun came from the porch and bullets whistled their deadly message in Lennister's ears as he gained the shelter of the trees.

He found his horse and was quickly in the saddle. When he passed the windbreak of cottonwoods, shielding him from the house, he took to the road below the fields and spurred his mount to the gate. He took the time to close the gate to delay pursuit and then struck straight across the fields toward the lower end of the bluffs.

Suddenly the deep-throated ranch bell pealed its warning message on the night air. Lennister reached the shadow of the bluffs and started up the steep slope. To the westward, where the bluffs met the bench land that reached northward, a glare lit up the sky and tongues of flame shot high.

Lennister topped the last rise and, driving in his spurs, dashed eastward on the plain, watching the blaze of the signal fire over his left shoulder.

CHAPTER TWENTY-TWO

Lennister was conscious of a certain grim feeling of satisfaction as he rode swiftly across the shadowy prairie on his way back to Rattle Butte and the rendezvous with Robbins and the Triangle men. He had at least convinced Graham that he meant business, and had dispelled any illusions the Bar Cross owner might have possessed as to the ease with which he would bring the Triangle and Connie Cameron, or her father, to time. There was a faint possibility that Graham, realizing what he was up against, would draw in his guns, although Lennister—convinced that Trope was really in command—doubted such a move.

But Graham had unwittingly showed that he was incensed toward Connie Cameron and jealous of her father. He was nettled, too, because he had not been asked to join the Teton association. Possibly he blamed Will Cameron for this, despite the fact that the Bar Cross was really south of the range governed by the association.

Lennister's suspicions that the matter of the range between the river in the north and Rattle Butte was not the cause of the trouble had proved well founded and his other surmises correct.

Furthermore, Lennister had satisfied himself that it would be necessary to protect the Triangle stock by such means as offered. Graham had ignored his reference to the driving south of the big Triangle herd as stealing it, and Lennister knew that such a charge would not hold. Trope had driven away the Bar Cross cattle. He could claim he didn't know the Triangle cattle were mixed with his, that he couldn't help it, and that the Triangle outfit was welcome to come and get its stock.

But Lennister knew if the Triangle beeves got on Bar Cross range south of Rattle Butte, it would be no end of trouble to get them back, and there were innumerable ways in which steers could be lost and reduced in weight—all of which would mean a financial loss to the Camerons. Lennister's thoughts now were chiefly concerned with the protecting of the Cameron property. It was, of course, the first duty of a ranch foreman, whether he was a permanent or only an acting foreman. Lennister had worked cattle, and he knew.

As he sped into the northeast toward the trees below the butte, Lennister saw a series of swift-moving shadows on the dim western plain. His practiced eye told him at once that the shadows were riders.

"The whole outfit is sloping for the ranch," he muttered.

It was true. The signal fire had attracted the Bar Cross men, who were riding to the home ranch with all the speed their mounts could muster. Lennister reflected that it must have been a prearranged precaution. The ringing of the ranch bell called for the lighting of the fire and the calling to the ranch of all Bar Cross men who saw it, a signal that there was trouble.

The riders moved on south, and Lennister changed his course so that he rode directly north toward the butte instead of northeast in a detour. When he was within a mile of the butte, he swerved east and rode to the trees below it. Here he crossed the little creek flowing from the springs and rode up it until a horseman broke out of cover ahead of him. It was Robbins.

"Most of 'em have gone south," said Robbins in guarded tones. "They didn't have a man on the butte, or else you fixed him. I went on the butte, and there is some sort of fire down there. . . ."

"I know," Lennister interrupted. "There was some trouble

down there." He paused and found himself wondering for the first time who it was he had had to shoot down to gain his liberty when caught between the cross-fire in the ranch house living room. "Anyway, their horses will be pretty well spent by the time they get there, and they'll have to round up fresh mounts to start back on." He was impatient. "That'll delay 'em, but we've got to work fast. Is the bunch here?"

Robbins gave a low whistle, and the Triangle riders began to emerge from the shadows of the trees.

"Split 'em in two groups," Lennister told Robbins crisply. "Take one group around below the butte, and I'll take the other around above. We want to get 'em by surprise. There's probably two or three riding herd on the cattle, and the cook, anyway, in the cabin. Don't do any shooting, you fellows, if you can help it."

Robbins divided the men, and the two factions rode swiftly around the butte. Lennister saw the herders first and closed in on them just beyond the trees between the cabin and the big herd. In a moment they were surrounded and disarmed—a surly trio who said nothing and obeyed silently when told to ride ahead through the trees toward the cabin.

At the cabin, Lennister found Robbins covering the cook and another man who was speedily disarmed. Then all five prisoners were herded into the cabin.

"Get the herd up," Lennister ordered Robbins. "We're going to move the cattle around to the east slope of the butte and drive 'em up there."

"On top?" said Robbins, rather stupidly.

"On top," snapped Lennister. "There's plenty of room up there for the herd. There's grass and water there. There's only one way to get up, and a handful of men can hold that slope against an army!"

Then Lennister took charge in earnest. Many of the steers

were already up off the ground and milling about uneasily. Soon all the cattle were in movement—a dark mass edging around north of the butte and up the long slope, guarded on either side by the buckbrush, the only means of reaching the big tableland on top of Rattle.

Lennister put three men to packing supplies from the cabin to the top of the butte where the Triangle range cook, who had brought down the extra horses in company with Joe Curley, soon was improvising a kitchen at the western end of the miniature lake.

Lennister did not expect the Bar Cross men to return speedily. Graham would, of course, immediately make known the fact that Lennister had been at the ranch. They would not expect concerted action so soon. Very likely they would send out pursuit parties to look in the bottoms and spread out in the north and east. Originally Lennister had planned a surprise attack on the Bar Cross outfit at the butte, but, as things had turned out, it was just as well, he thought.

He did not relish the thought of the shooting at the ranch, but it would have meant death to have stayed in that room with two men shooting at him—with others on the way to help. He had promised Connie Cameron to keep his gun cold unless— well, that had been a time when a cold gun would have cut short his efforts in her behalf. And he hadn't shot to kill—there was that consolation. He shook his head in irritation and went about his tasks.

What was the matter with him? Was he getting soft—and over this girl?

The moon thrust its disk of silver above the eastern horizon and aided them in their work. The herd was a moving blot, surging around the butte and up the slope. The supplies and then the prisoners were taken up, and Lennister stationed a man at the southern edge of the great tableland to watch for the anticipated return of the Bar Cross outfit.

But the first gray of the dawn came, and no riders appeared from the south. Lennister was at a loss to understand it, unless it could be that there were no fresh horses immediately available at the Bar Cross, or that the men had been told to remain there and go back in the morning. At all events, the fact that Trope's outfit hadn't shown itself indicated that they were content to let the herd remain at Rattle Butte for the time being.

The sun was up and the last of the cattle were being driven up the slope to the tableland when the look-out announced that a lone rider was coming at a furious pace from the direction of the Bar Cross. Lennister rode out west of the butte and soon saw that the horseman was not heading for the butte but was going on north as fast as his horse could carry him. Lennister put the spurs to his fresh mount and galloped west to head off the mysterious horseman.

The rider saw him coming and turned a bit east to meet him, evidently thinking he was one of the Bar Cross herders who had been left with the cattle. When he discovered his mistake, he veered off, but he was too late, and Lennister closed in on him with his gun ready for any emergency.

"Where to, with such energy, so early in the morning?" Lennister inquired, noting the man's hard face and cruel eyes. This rider was typical in appearance with the men of Trope's outfit. Most of them had been brought in by Trope himself, Lennister had heard, and the fact seemed significant.

"I'm on my way to the Triangle," was the surly reply.

"Yes . . . and why?" drawled Lennister.

"I ain't got no orders to tell you," said the man with a black look.

Lennister appeared interested. "I'm glad to know you're under orders and not on your own hook," he said meaningfully.

"But I'm bossing the Triangle right at present, and I reckon, if you want to jog on up there, you'll have to tell me the lay."

The man seemed puzzled by Lennister's presence there and kept looking toward Rattle Butte where, by this time, not a head of stock was to be seen. His perplexity increased until he blurted: "Where'd the cattle go?"

"You haven't answered my question," Lennister reminded him.

"Oh. . . ." The man's speech trailed off in an oath. "You made off with the cattle, eh?" he said with a shrewd look. "Well, you'll. . . ."

"You don't figure to answer my question, I reckon," said Lennister, reaching over and jerking the man's gun out of its holster while he kept him covered. "All right, swing over this way with me and we'll keep you handy."

"I tell you. . . ." The man hesitated, working his lips savagely. "Look at this," he said finally. "I'm taking it to the Triangle."

He held out an envelope that he took from inside his shirt. Lennister took it and glanced at the inscription. It was addressed to **Miss Connie Cameron, Triangle Ranch.**

Lennister handed it back. "Who from?" he demanded sternly.

"From the old man, since you got to know everything," was the sneering reply. "Graham told me to beat it up there as quick as I could, or sooner, an' give it to the party it's addressed to."

"All right. We'll drop over by the butte for a minute and then I'll go with you. It might be one of those clever Bar Cross tricks," he finished with a sharp look at the messenger.

"I ain't got much time," the man grumbled. "It's important."

"No doubt. Do you know what's in it?"

"Maybe I've got an idea an' maybe I ain't. But I ain't goin' to tell you, Mister Gunfighter."

"It doesn't make much difference since it isn't addressed to me," said Lennister, motioning the messenger to precede him on the way to the butte, and ignoring what the other had sarcastically called him. "But I know one thing, and that's that you're sure going to deliver it."

Robbins, who had been watching from the trees near the butte, came riding out to meet him.

Lennister drew him aside and quickly explained.

"When you have all the cattle up there, start cutting out the Bar Cross brand and drive 'em down," he instructed at parting. "Keep the Triangle herd up there and hold the butte."

A minute later he was riding at a fast gallop for the Triangle, with Graham's messenger.

CHAPTER TWENTY-THREE

There was little said on that ride from Rattle Butte to the Triangle. The Bar Cross messenger kept darting surreptitious glances at Lennister, but the latter paid no attention to him whatever. It was plain to Lennister, however, that the man knew who he was, that Trope had doubtless spread his description among his outfit, probably with certain definite instructions and warnings. There were questions Lennister would have liked to ask the man, but he realized that would do little good, since he could hardly compel the man to answer under the circumstances, or depend on the answers he might make.

Thus they rode in silence, Lennister retaining possession of the messenger's weapon, and watching him covertly. It lacked an hour and a half of noon when they arrived at the Triangle and dismounted in the courtyard, turning the horses over to one of the wounded men there who was able to get about and look after the barn.

Lennister led the way to the front of the house and Connie Cameron came out the front door as they reached the steps.

Lennister met her look of surprise with a warning contraction of his brows. "This man comes from the Bar Cross," he explained, "and brings a letter he says is from Graham."

The messenger fumbled at his shirt, forgetting to take off his hat, and finally handed up the envelope.

"We'll go into the office," Connie decided, leading the way into the house.

She sat down at her father's desk while the messenger stood just within the door with Lennister a step behind him.

Connie broke open the envelope, took out a sheet of note paper, and quickly scanned what was written upon it. Lennister saw her hands tremble and her face go white. When she lifted her eyes, it was not to look at the messenger, but at him, and he thought her gaze was brimming with disappointment and accusation. She read the note a second time, and then crumpled it in her hand.

"You will go to the bunkhouse and wait until everything is ready for you to start back," she told the messenger. "Your horse will need some rest, and I'll have something sent out to you to eat." Her tone was not hospitable, and she rose impulsively as the man went out.

"Why . . . why did you do it?" she said with a catch in her voice as she looked steadily at Lennister and tossed the crumpled note before him on the table.

He picked it up calmly, smoothed it out, and read:

Miss Cameron,

Your man Lennister broke into my house last night and shot Claude. I have sent to town for the doctor, but I understand that the physician was at your place and may still be there. If he is there, maybe you will be human enough to send him back with my man. I congratulate you on having a man so ready to carry out your orders.

Frank Graham

Lennister also read the note twice. Claude! Her orders? His eyes narrowed and flashed. So Claude was the one who had come to the door shooting, and Graham was sufficiently mean and despicable to convey the impression that he believed Connie Cameron had sent Lennister to the Bar Cross to shoot Claude Graham.

160

"Miss Connie, do you believe that?" Lennister asked slowly.

"Isn't it true?" she countered in an unsteady voice.

"I reckon I didn't ask just the question I had in mind . . . I mean . . . well, ma'am, it's true I shot a man there last night."

"After promising me what you did?" she said dully.

"I don't remember promising thataway," he protested. "I want to ask one thing, Miss Cameron, before I say any more. Do you trust me at all? If you didn't trust me, why did you send for me?"

"But . . . but after this," she faltered. "I shouldn't have told you about that silly business with Claude," she continued with spirit. "I might have known. What will people say? They all know in town that Claude and I had a difference at the dance, and that it nearly brought about a clash between the Bar Cross and the Triangle. Now they'll say I sent for you to come and shoot Claude."

She seemed on the verge of tears, and Lennister's face was an unnatural gray through its coating of healthy tan.

"And it might be hard to prove that they lie," he said, "but I want *you* to know the truth first. I went down there to see Graham and maybe find out a few things by the way he talked. I got what I wanted, and I know that it's jealousy and not the north range that's bothering him. And I know Trope's got him between thumb and finger and that it's Trope we're fighting."

"Just how does that help matters any?" she asked in a stronger voice. "Oh, if father could only speak . . . could only tell who shot him."

"He will, sooner or later," Lennister reassured her. "At the end of our talk Graham pulled out a whistle and blew it. I tried to stop him, and we went to the floor. He got up and blew out the light. Then the shooting started with him blazing at me there in the dark room. Somebody came down the stairs and, when I tried to get out the door, a gun was spitting fire in my face and another was barking behind my back. I shot the man in the door high on the right . . . to stop him. I knocked another down on the porch. Then I beat it with bullets playing a tune on the wind. I had little time to think, ma'am, and I didn't know that man in the door was Claude. If I'd known it was him, I might have stood and taken it on your account."

For the space of a minute she looked at him steadily, and finally he saw that she believed him.

"Oh, Lennister," she said tremulously as she sank into a chair. "Can't . . . can't troubles like this be settled without bloodshed?"

"Not when there is a man like Trope mixed up in it, Miss Connie. I thought I might be able to scare Graham out of it, but Trope's got him buffaloed into thinking that his gun makes right, I reckon. I know the breed, ma'am. He's more dangerous than an out-and-out killer, for he's under cover . . . Trope, I mean. I'm afraid I'm going to have to meet Trope, Miss Connie, if I stay on the job."

She looked at him startled. "I . . . don't want. . . ." Her speech died away before the grim expression in his eyes.

"If I leave, Miss Connie, they'll ride you to death," he continued gravely. "I started with the idea that I could make it by taking 'em by surprise and getting the cattle back that way. But it looks worse at every turn. Graham wants certain social readjustments, I take it, and he wants your dad under his submission. Trope wants to teach the Triangle a lesson, as I suppose he looks at it, and I wouldn't be surprised if he wanted more than that. I wouldn't put it past Trope to run off those beeves with those cut-throats he's got working for him . . . if he could. A man like that will play any kind of a game, ma'am."

The girl's eyes were flashing again. "He shot my father!" she exclaimed. "I know it . . . I just know it."

"Whoever shot him shot to kill," said Lennister soberly. Then, as Connie's eyes clouded again: "I'm just trying to show you the situation," he said hastily. "I'm afraid my coming hasn't helped things any so far as Trope is concerned. After all that's happened, Graham might quit. But Trope hates me worse than poison since I've butted into his game. *He* won't stop, and if I leave, he won't forget I was here."

Lennister's words carried regret, and the girl saw a new expression on his face that caused her to wonder.

"Where are the men?" she asked.

"At Rattle Butte. We drove the cattle to the top of the butte this morning. I told Robbins to cut out the Bar Cross brands up there and drive 'em down, but to keep the Triangle stuff there till we get a chance to move 'em back up this way. The butte is on Blue Dome range, Miss Connie, and if you wanted to put it up to the association, I reckon they'd see that the cattle got back all right."

"Father wouldn't appeal to the association, and *I* won't," she said with spirit. "I'll wait until he can talk again, anyway. The doctor says he should be out of his delirium tonight, and then after he has had some sleep he can talk just a little. He would never forgive me if I went against his wishes while he is helpless."

"Then I reckon we'd better think it over after dinner," said Lennister in a tired voice. "I'm going to the bunkhouse for an hour's sleep, since I missed out last night and had only a half ration the night before."

He smiled wanly, and the girl put a hand on his arm.

"Lennister, I *do* believe you and . . . trust you," she said softly, and then hurried down the hall.

When he awoke, he found he had slept four hours, and it that was nearly 3:00 P.M. He got out of his bunk hurriedly, noting that the Bar Cross messenger, who had been there when he had entered, had gone.

Connie Cameron called to him from the kitchen door when he went into the courtyard.

"Come in, I've kept some dinner for you," she said cheerfully.

When he had finished eating, she came in and told him that her father was sleeping and had passed the crisis.

"The doctor will be back from the Bar Cross this evening. He went with the man who brought the note right after dinner."

She had hardly finished speaking when the thunder of hoofs came from the bench trail and a number of riders dashed into the courtyard. They both moved swiftly to the window and saw Sheriff Strang dismounting.

CHAPTER TWENTY-FOUR

Connie looked quickly at Lennister with apprehension. His eyes had narrowed, and his gaze was steel-blue. There was just a flash of that terrible look of which she knew he was capable, and of which she was afraid. It was like playing with fire—trying to handle this man.

"I reckon they're after me," he said in a low, grim tone.

"Wait!" she said, grasping his arm. "You stay here and let me talk to him. Do as I say, Lennister, it's . . . it's orders."

He remained standing back from the window with his face toward the door where she disappeared into the hall. He heard her greet the sheriff and take him into the little front office. He moved to the door where he could hear what was said. For some moments after they entered the office there was silence, then: "Miss Cameron, I didn't think you would do a thing like this," said the sheriff in his official voice.

"Like what, Sheriff?" the girl asked, almost impudently.

"We can't take this lightly, Miss Cameron," said Strang severely. "It is a serious matter. I thought it was funny . . . you sending for this gunman, Lennister . . . but I didn't think you had enough of a grudge against Claude Graham to send for a gunfighter to get him."

Lennister could imagine the angry flush on Connie's face.

"You think I did that, Sheriff?" she asked quietly.

"Everything points that way." There was no uncertainty or uneasiness in Strang's voice this day. "Anyway, the thing has been done and . . . you said you would be responsible. I shall have to hold you responsible with Lennister."

"Suppose you hold me and me alone responsible," was the girl's astonishing retort.

"I see that you don't deny the . . . the complication," said Strang. "Well, perhaps that's best. Anyone hereabouts will sympathize with you, Miss Cameron, considering the worry you have had and your state of mind. It may be that this fellow, Lennister, has taken advantage of you. In fact, I believe that's just about the way of it."

"No one has taken advantage of me, Sheriff," said Connie coldly, "unless it is Graham and his outfit. And I'm not looking for sympathy. What is your business here?"

"I want Lennister and . . . I guess it will be necessary for you to drop into town, too, Miss Cameron. Oh, not today, of course, but someday when your father is better."

"Has Graham made another complaint?" asked the girl sweetly.

"He has, and I can't say that I blame him," replied Strang sternly. "When a man breaks into another's house and shoots. . . ."

"Lennister didn't break into any house," Connie broke in impatiently. "He went down there to try to reason with Graham. While they were talking, Graham blew a whistle, put the light out, and started shooting at Lennister. Then a man came downstairs to the door and started shooting, also. Lennister only shot once, and he didn't know it was Claude, or he probably wouldn't have shot at all. What would you do if you were caught in a room with two men peppering away at you with their guns?"

"That's a pretty story, but that's about all," said Strang in a tone of irritation. "I suppose Lennister came back and told that as his alibi?"

"Yes. Lennister told me that," Connie affirmed.

"Assuming that you didn't send him down there to shoot Claude," said the sheriff, clearing his throat officiously, "do you believe him?"

"I do," answered the girl stoutly.

"Then neither he nor you deny that he shot Claude Graham?"

"We don't deny it," replied Connie after a moment's pause.

For the space of half a minute there was silence, and the frown on Lennister's face darkened. He shifted from one foot to the other uneasily, and listened.

"I think it'd be best if you went into town and made a deposition to that effect, Miss Cameron," the sheriff said at length.

"What . . . now? Today?" The girl's tone was startled.

"In the absence of Lennister . . . yes," replied Strang.

Lennister stepped quickly through the door and down the hall to the door of the office. Strang leaped to his feet and jerked out his gun.

"It won't be necessary, Sheriff," said Lennister calmly, "I'm not absent." He looked with a glimmer of amusement in his eyes at the gun in the sheriff's hand. "You might as well put that up, Sheriff; you look awkward, holding it thataway."

"You're my prisoner!" Strang blurted. "I want you."

"So I gathered from your remarks," said Lennister dryly. "There's only one thing, Sheriff." His look changed on the instant. "I'll go along with you on one condition, and that's that you leave Miss Cameron out of it. Understand? Out of it entirely."

"You're taking the blame then," said Strang with a scowl. "I dare say it'll be where it belongs."

"You've said it," said Lennister whimsically. "I'm taking the blame. It's up to you to prove the rest of it. You're all wrong, Sheriff, when you say that Miss Connie sent me down there.

She didn't. She didn't know I was going. I went down there to see Graham, and the rest of it happened. That's enough for you. Does it let her out?" The question came like the crack of a whiplash.

Strang looked at him for some moments. "Yes, it lets her out," he said at last.

"Clear out?" Lennister persisted.

"Clear out," snapped Strang. "You have my word for it."

With a swift movement that caused the sheriff to raise his gun quickly, Lennister unbuckled his gun belt and laid it with its weapon on the table.

"Lennister!" It was Connie Cameron, but she caught herself and turned to the sheriff with a white face. "He is still in my employ . . . *our* employ," she said spiritedly. "How much is his bail?"

Strang smiled a grim, cheerless smile. "It'll be as high as I can get 'em to make it," he said. "Five thousand, anyway . . . and cash. That's providing I can't get them to hold him."

"But Claude isn't seriously shot, and he was shot in another county," Connie contended.

Strang shook his head. "The Bar Cross ranch house itself is in the dip in the southwest corner of Blue Dome County," he declared. "Most of the Bar Cross range isn't, but the house is. And we don't know how bad young Graham is shot, yet." He gathered up Lennister's belt and gun.

"Are you ready?" he asked sternly.

"Any time," replied Lennister, and his smile caused the sheriff to watch him carefully as they joined the posse in the courtyard and waited until a man brought his horse.

Lennister looked back at Connie Cameron just once as she stood on the porch and smiled at her.

She watched them ride up the road to the bench and disappear in a cloud of dust. After they had gone, and the dust cloud had dissolved, and the place was once more quiet save for the breathing of the wind in the cottonwoods, she still stood staring at the blue rim of the sky. Finally she went into the office.

For a spell she stood by the table, tapping its surface listlessly. Then she sat down in her father's swivel chair. She had a feeling that she was utterly and completely alone. But she did not feel sorry for herself, nor did she feel any particular interest in the affairs of the ranch at that moment. It was of Lennister's smile that she thought—and the look in his eyes. Little as she understood him, she could realize what the loss of his liberty had meant to him. If it hadn't been that he wanted to protect her, she doubted if the sheriff and all his men could have taken him. She had sent for him, and it had come to this. She believed him when he said he had tried to keep from using his gun. She trusted him now. $5,000. Connie came to herself with a start. Her gaze had been centered on the small safe in the office beside the desk. She looked around almost furtively. In that safe was $5,000 belonging to the Teton Stockmen's Association. $10,000 had been placed there some time before to cover the rewards for the capture of Blodgett and his rustling band. It had been Lennister who had broken up the band and disposed of Blodgett. But he had taken only $5,000. The money had since reposed in the safe. In a way it really had belonged to him. Joe Curley had said something about having heard that Lennister had had a run of hard luck in the town in the north—lost a lot of money in some way, cards perhaps. His $5,000 was doubtless almost gone. He was entitled to be bailed out of jail with the $5,000 he could have had for the asking, she argued to herself. And, anyway, she—her father or the Triangle—were good for the money. Why not?

The idea disturbed her, kept her thinking until the arrival of the doctor at dinner time. He brought the news that Claude

Graham was hit in the shoulder and that it was not serious. Connie remembered that Lennister had said he had shot high on the right and her heart sang.

After supper the doctor told her that it was his intention to drive back to town.

"Your father will be rational when he wakes up," he told her, "and the housekeeper knows what to do. Feed him light and let him rest . . . that's the prescription. I'll be out again tomorrow to look in on him. And, listen, Connie . . ."—he patted her on the shoulder—"I guess I've got some news you'll be glad to hear. It's about Claude Graham. He's sorry, child . . . very sorry. He made me promise to tell you so. He said he meant it, too, when he came up here yesterday morning to see you . . . meant that he wanted to help you because he was ashamed of the way he'd acted in town, but he guessed he didn't use the right words."

Connie felt something swell in her throat as she listened.

"He isn't all bad," the doctor continued. "I guess that fellow Trope has had a bad influence over him. He told me this in snatches, as if he was afraid somebody there would hear him. He said his father had some queer ideas, but that he was going to tell him a few things." The doctor nodded wisely. "Acted right spirited," he declared. "Made me promise not to tell anybody but you, Miss Connie, and then whispered in my ear that Lennister wasn't to blame. Said he'd try to make it right soon as he got everything straight, and to tell you he was sorry, and I guess he is, if I know anything about humans."

Connie bade him good bye with shining eyes and went up to find that her father was sleeping peacefully.

The man from the Bar Cross, who had ridden back with the doctor as a courtesy to the physician from Graham, finished his supper in the deserted bunkhouse and strolled under the trees, smoking, preparatory to going back to the ranch in the south.

Connie Cameron came out on the porch and stood for some time, staring, unseeing, at the last crimson gleams of the sunset. Lennister wasn't to blame! Of course not! He had as much as said so himself, and she had believed him. She was glad of that. He *had* tried to keep his gun cold, had risked his life in the effort to keep his promise to her. And he had taken all the blame to protect her. True, that was no more than right under the circumstances, but another kind of man would have found it easy to evade it.

"I'm going to get Lennister back!" she involuntarily exclaimed aloud.

She hurried into the house and quickly changed into her riding clothes. Then, making sure that the housekeeper did not see her, she slipped down to the little office and closed the door. There was just enough light so that she could see the combination dial of the safe. She turned the dial rapidly, her breath coming fast. At last the door of the safe swung open. She drew out a packet and thrust it within her jacket. As she closed the safe, a shadow moved from the window toward the corral, where a saddled horse was standing, and soon the horse was bearing a rider west through the fields in the bottoms.

CHAPTER TWENTY-FIVE

Dusk had fallen, and the sky was sprinkled with stars, when Connie Cameron rode out upon the bench and headed for Ransford. Her mount was fresh and eager, the air was cool and stimulating, and there was a wild exultation in her heart. Every fiber of her healthy young body—every nerve—responded to the cut of the crisp wind, the rhythmic play of her horse's muscles, the beauty of the calm prairie night. It was like drifting through a fairyland of starlight and shadow, and the white tracks of the road were like silver rails leading to some mysterious happy haven.

She thrilled with the thought that she was bent on a mission that concerned a man's liberty. To turn Lennister out under the stars he loved! Could a man be thoroughly bad and love the perfume of lilacs? She knew better. That last look out of the gray eyes as he had waved farewell had told her much, after all. She felt thrilled, strangely light-hearted, exhilarated with her own thoughts, and she tossed contemplation of the reason for them to the scented night wind and rode on.

Some five miles from the ranch house the road swung down toward the river, where it was joined by another road from the south. There were a few cottonwoods at this place—tall, graceful shadows with their tops weaving among the stars, it seemed.

As she neared this spot, where the road turned sharply into the northwest and led directly to town, she peered ahead with more than ordinary attentiveness. She could see between the trunks of the trees, and yet she would have been ready to swear she had seen one of those trees move. It moved again—two of them moved! But no—it wasn't the trees. There were other shadows there. And then she swerved sharply to the right, out of the road—but too late.

The shadows came hurtling out from under the branches, and she saw the sharp outlines of two horses and riders. Her spurs sank into the flanks of her horse, and the gallant animal lunged ahead, but the shadows crossed before her and closed in. Her horse snorted and shied from one side to the other, and then slowed down as the riders swung in abruptly and one of them leaned from his saddle and caught her bridle rein.

With all her might Connie brought her quirt down upon the man's forearm and drew a curse. She felt herself grasped about the waist, and next instant she was dragged from the saddle and was held, despite her struggles, against the saddle and leg of the other rider. She struck out to no avail, and sobbed with the thought that she had no weapon.

The other rider had dismounted, and now he came running to the assistance of his companion. He took her in a grip of iron, pinned her arms to her sides, while his companion flung himself from his horse, tore open her jacket, and secured the package of bills she had taken from the Triangle safe. She caught a glimpse of their faces, and saw that they were masked with handkerchiefs.

The man who held her suddenly flung her to the ground. She rose with a choking cry of angry despair. Her assailants were in their saddles, riding away. She stood helpless, white-faced, her hands clenched so hard that the knuckles were white, and watched the robbers disappear beyond the cottonwoods. The sharp echoes of flying hoofs dulled, died away, and the night was still.

For just one minute Connie remained standing there, a mist

in her eyes, then she mastered the impulse to cry with chagrin—to call futilely for help. The thing had been done—and not a word had been spoken. Someone must have known, of course. And next she remembered the Bar Cross man who had accompanied the doctor back to the Triangle. She hadn't seen him since before supper. But he might have walked about at will, for there were but two men at the ranch—the slightly wounded man who was looking after the barn, and the other wounded man who was lying in the bunkhouse. She bit her lip in perplexity as she went to her horse and mounted. The second man could not be accounted for unless—no, the man with the doctor had had no companion.

She turned back to the ranch, for there was no use in going into town without the cash with which to give bond for Lennister. It would gain her nothing to go in and report the robbery. And suddenly she was struck by the realization that she didn't want anyone to know of the robbery. It wasn't Triangle money she had taken. Her imagination and excited reasoning had caused her to think she had a right to take it for the purpose she had in mind. But how could she explain it? Her father would have to know when he was better. He would understand and attend to it. The Triangle would have to pay it, of course. A lump came into Connie's throat.

She put her horse in the barn, and, when she entered the house, the housekeeper was startled by her pallor.

"Out riding, but too soon to suit my supper," she explained lamely. Then, to change the subject: "How is Father?"

"He's awake," replied the housekeeper. "You'd better go to bed, dearie. That's a good girl. You've had too much to think about."

But Connie disregarded the elder woman's advice and hurried up to her father's room.

Her father lay motionlessly in the great, white bed, the soft rays of the shaded lamp lending a mother-of-pearl transparency to his face. His eyes turned to Connie as she went to the bedside, bent over, and kissed his forehead. She stroked his hands and smoothed the pillows and coverings. He kept his eyes on her—great, glowing orbs full of meaning under the white bandage about his head. Then he opened his mouth and she bent low to catch the murmured words.

"Trope . . . shot . . . me."

Connie straightened with a flash in her eyes. Then she put a cool finger against his lips.

"Yes, Daddy," she soothed. "We know. But everything is all right. You must rest and get strong, and not think about it now."

His eyes fastened on hers imploringly. "The . . . cattle?" he whispered.

"They are all safe," said Connie. "Robbins has our herd intact. There is nothing to worry over or think about now, Daddy. Just close your eyes and rest . . . *please*, Daddy."

Her father did close his eyes while she sat by the bedside, holding one of his hands. Soon his regular breathing told her that he was again asleep. The housekeeper came in to take up her vigil, and Connie went out.

On the little balcony over the porch Connie stood, looking at the stars, and thinking—thinking.

It seemed to her that her brain was growing numb with her problem. Every instinct of her wild young nature—reverted now to the primitive instincts she had inherited—was aroused. It *had* been Trope who had shot her father; it had been Trope who had filed the complaints with the sheriff; it had been Trope, doubtless, who had instigated Claude Graham's visit to the dance hall; it had been Trope who had threatened the Triangle men in town that night. What would his next move be? And now the $5,000 had been stolen and she had every reason to believe that a Bar Cross man was the thief. Trope himself might be implicated. And she was alone on the ranch. She had felt safe, secure with Lennister in charge. He understood. To whom could she turn now?

She heard a horse canter into the courtyard, and, looking down from the end of the balcony, saw a rider dismounting. She hurried down to find Joe Curley approaching the kitchen door. She invited him in, and at once noticed his grave face—its wrinkles showing deeper than ever, the eyes worried and tired.

"Robbins sent me," he explained. "We cut out the Bar Cross brand an' drove 'em down on the prairie. The Triangle herd is on top the butte. Graham sent word we could move our cattle north. Robbins thinks it's a trick, because the whole Bar Cross outfit, almost, is camped east of the butte. I had to sneak away to get up here. Where's Lennister?"

Connie thought rapidly. To send word that Lennister had been taken by the sheriff might dishearten Robbins and the others. She did not know what to think of Graham's message. Had Claude exercised whatever influence he had with his father? The presence of the Bar Cross outfit there did not look good. It might be a trick, as Robbins suspected. Connie stared at the little wrangler as her thoughts raced to a daring conclusion.

"Robbins was wondering when Lennister would be back," Joe said uneasily.

"Tell him that Lennister will be back in the morning," said Connie slowly. "Tell him not to move the cattle until Lennister comes."

"I'll be hurrying back, Miss Connie," said Joe simply.

Connie saw to it that he got a fresh mount, then she went into the house again and stole upstairs to her father's room. He was asleep, and the housekeeper was lying on a cot that had been put in the room for her accommodation. She seemed asleep, also, and Connie tiptoed to the closet, took down her father's gun belt and weapon, and slipped out of the room.

In the office downstairs, Connie took the cartridges out of the belt and put them in her pockets. Then she strapped the big weapon under her jacket and left the house. For the second time that night she rode up the bench trail and started for Ransford. She did not follow the road this time, but cut straight across the prairie, keeping the rising moon at her back, in an airline for town.

The gun pressed against her side cruelly as she rode, and finally she took it out and held it in her hand as she sped on her way. It was past midnight when she finally caught a faint glimmer of a light far ahead and saw the shadow of the cottonwoods about Ransford. Her heart came into her throat as she raced toward her goal. Could she do it? Could she hold up the sheriff or jailer and compel the release of Lennister? For the first time since she had made her resolve to free him by the only means that offered, she felt a numbing sense of misgiving. Could she do it? The question rang in her mind to the pound of her horse's hoofs. And then she reached the road, where it crossed the stream and ended in the short street of the town.

She concealed the gun quickly within her jacket and rode, without looking to either side, to the hotel barn. There she left her horse with instructions not to remove the saddle. She wanted to rest the animal, and to have time in which to think. She went into the hotel, dimly lit by a single lamp in the small lobby, and turned into the dark, deserted parlor. There she sat in a chair by the window, where she could look up the street.

Light flowed from the windows of the Rodeo resort and another place that she surmised was a small café. Otherwise the street was dark. She could not see the jail, which was at the upper end of the street, set back somewhat from the line of buildings.

For an hour she sat there, going over her plans, and then her pale face was lit by a faint smile. Lennister would know what to do.

Another hour she waited, and then she stole out and around to the barn. The barn man was not about—sleeping, probably, in the little front office. She made her way in the dim light to Spot's stall, spoke to him, and led him out. She tightened the saddle cinch and mounted. Avoiding the street, she picked her way along behind the buildings until she was at the upper end. In the shadow of the east side of the last building she dismounted and left Spot's reins dangling so he would stand. The jail was on the opposite side of the street.

She made her way to it and boldly entered the lighted office. One man was there, sitting in a chair with his feet propped on the desk. He got to his feet with a startled exclamation as she came in. He wasn't the sheriff, she saw at a glance, a deputy or the jailer, likely.

"I wish to speak for a few moments with my acting foreman, Lennister," she said coolly. "I am Miss Cameron of the Triangle. It is . . . ranch business."

The man removed his hat a bit awkwardly. "I . . . don't know about that, Miss Cameron. The sheriff left orders that nobody was to see your man."

"I hardly believe the sheriff had any idea *I* would come to see him," said Connie with a winning smile. "I told the sheriff, though, I intended to bail him out. Father has recovered consciousness, and it is necessary that I consult with Lennister. I won't be a minute," she added in a pleading tone.

The jailer frowned. He had a great deal of respect for Will Cameron's position in the community, and Connie's smile and supplicating voice were hard to resist.

"You want to see him alone, I suppose?" It seemed a senseless question, yet he had to be careful.

"For just a minute," said Connie sweetly. "But I don't have to go into his . . . his cell, of course. You could leave the door open. There . . . there has been some new trouble," she said in a different tone, which signified that she was at her wits' end. "I . . . I want his advice." She seemed on the point of tears, and the jailer stepped hastily forward.

As he swung his keys and moved toward the door leading into the jail proper, Connie thanked her stars for the experience she had had in amateur theatricals at school.

But he hesitated at the door. She had followed him with an eager look in her eyes. "I *thought* you would be kind enough," she said. "Afterward, I will be at the hotel until the morning, if the sheriff wants to see me, and I suppose he will."

Her trusting voice and earnest look decided the jailer, and the door swung open.

"In the corner cell," he said, pointing along the corridor.

Connie hurried to the cell as Lennister rose from the bunk and stepped to the barred door.

"Robbins doesn't know what to do with the cattle down there," she began hurriedly, but a hasty look over her shoulder showed that the jailer had stepped back into the front office.

Her hand went through the bars to grip Lennister's. He was looking at her in wonder. Then she spoke swiftly, telling him about Claude's message, of the word Robbins had sent, and last the loss of the $5,000.

"It will be all right about you," she whispered finally. "But we're losing time. They are up to some trick down there. You must get out . . . do you hear, Lennister?" Her breath came in short gasps in her excitement. "You . . . must get out."

She was taking the cartridges from her pockets, cramming them into his hands. Then, after a quick glance down the corridor, she took out the gun and passed it to him. Instantly it was inside his shirt. No one knew. The few other prisoners were in the other part of the jail; the jailer was in the office.

"My horse is across the street at the side of a building," she whispered.

"Go to the hotel and wait for me," he told her in a low voice. "Do as I say, Connie."

She nodded, looked at him breathlessly for a spell, then hurried along the corridor and out into the office.

"Thank you," she said to the jailer with a smile. "Now I'm going to the hotel."

He opened the street door to let her out.

CHAPTER TWENTY-SIX

The jailer came into the corridor, and Lennister called to him softly. He walked down to Lennister's cell and inspected him curiously for the third time since midnight, when the sheriff had left him in charge of the jail.

"There's a right smart breeze drifting in through that window up there," said Lennister, pointing to the open window in the wall at the end of the corridor. "I reckon his nibs, the sheriff, wouldn't want his pet prisoner to catch cold." He grinned affably.

The jailer took a pole in the corner and closed the window. Then he turned back to the cell, and as Lennister retreated to the farther end, he drew close against the bars—something he had been careful not to do on his previous visits.

"Listen, friend," said Lennister, turning and holding the other's gaze with his eyes. "Before you can step away from that door, I can drop you. Reach through with your keys, and beat it."

The jailer's jaw dropped and his eyes bulged with astonishment. He was unable to move in the moment of complete surprise.

"Sure," he mumbled finally, with a grin he meant to be mirthful. "Easiest thing in the world to get out of here." He laughed shortly, holding to the bars with both hands and peering with a puzzled frown at Lennister, who stood with his hands on his hips.

Lennister smiled, too. Then he began to pace back and forth at the rear of the cell while the jailer eyed him steadily, a captive to his insatiable curiosity concerning this man of such a sinister reputation.

On his third turn Lennister suddenly whirled, and his hand came out from within his shirt holding the gun Connie Cameron had brought him. Its black muzzle covered the jailer as Lennister spoke in a low, hissing voice.

"I mean it. Don't move."

The jailer might have been paralyzed so far as he was capable of movement at that moment. He saw only the gun and Lennister's gleaming eyes above it, the narrowed lids, the stern set of the chin, thought only of what he had heard—what the sheriff had told him—that Lennister was desperate, dangerous, and a killer.

Lennister stepped swiftly toward him. "Don't take your hands from those bars!" he commanded. "I'm going out of here, my friend, and you might as well take it sensibly. I reckon if you've got any brains at all, now's a good time to use 'em."

Keeping the jailer covered, he reached through and took his keys, tearing the chain to which they were attached free from his belt. He stepped back, and in the wink of an eye had transferred the gun to his left hand, the keys to his right. He chose one he had noticed in particular when he had been locked in. It would have been hard to forget that key.

"Step back two paces," Lennister ordered sharply. "Honest, fellow, if you start down that corridor, I'll let you have it."

The jailer's face was pale as he obeyed. It was plain that he was more frightened than chagrined or worried over what the sheriff might say or do.

Lennister reached through the bars with his right hand, inserted the key in the primitive lock, and turned it. Next the cell door swung open, and he stepped lightly into the corridor.

He motioned to the jailer with his gun.

"Get in there," he snapped. "Do you hear me?"

The jailer sidled into the cell and Lennister closed the door and locked it, thrusting the keys in his pocket. Then, having learned just how it was done, he took the pole from the corner of the corridor near the cell, walked around to the other side, and closed the other windows. Then he returned to the cell, where the jailer, angry and belligerent now, stood glaring through the bars.

"I trusted that girl," the jailer blurted.

"Fair enough," said Lennister. "You don't know all the circumstances. The sheriff doesn't know 'em. This game is too deep for you *hombres*. Time counts, and that's why I've got to do this. Now with those windows closed and the doors shut, you can just naturally yell your head off without it doing you a speck of good. So long."

He went out the door into the office, closing it and locking it after him. A quick inspection of the drawers of the desk revealed his own gun belt and weapon. He put them on. Then he slipped out the door into the street, crossed to the opposite side, mounted Connie's horse, and rode back down behind the buildings on that side.

Connie Cameron—her thoughts torn between elation and dire misgiving—waited nervously in the darkened parlor of the hotel. Would Lennister get out? Would he shoot down the jailer? She shuddered at the thought. But she didn't believe he would adopt such a drastic measure. She was wise enough to construct in her own mind just such a scene as actually took place within the jail. She believed Lennister would get out, that he would hurry to the butte to direct things there, and that, in some way, he would recover the association's $5,000. She flushed as she considered the extent to which she depended on this acknowledged gunman, and the trust she reposed in him. And then there came a tapping at the window.

She looked out and recognized Lennister's tall form at once. She hurried out of the deserted lobby, and joined him at the side of the building. Without a word he took her arm and led her toward the barn, past it into the cottonwoods. There she found two horses, her own and—Lennister's.

"You forgot that I rode in," whispered Lennister. "The sheriff put my horse in the barn. I got him out and saddled him without waking the barn man. Climb up and follow me."

Connie's breath came fast with excitement as they walked their horses through the trees to the upper end of town and crossed the creek. Then, with the screen of cottonwoods to the right of them, Lennister led the way to the southeast, across the moonlit reaches of prairie.

He set a fast pace, and they rode silently, save for the dull sounds of the flying hoofs in the bunch grass. Connie shook off her misgivings. Let the sheriff take what action he saw fit. He would know, of course, when he heard the jailer's story, that she had brought the gun to Lennister. Little she cared. With her father abed as the result of Trope's bullet, with the cattle still threatened—a thousand head of beef steers at stake—and with $5,000 stolen, what other course should she have pursued? To expect action from the authorities was foolish. To appeal to the association would take time and allow Trope to put through any scheme he had in mind.

They arrived at the junction of the road from the ranch and the other from the south. Lennister drew rein.

"You'd best go on to the ranch, Miss Connie," he told her.

Connie looked at his stern face in the moonlight. "Where are you going, Lennister?" she asked, although she knew what his answer would be.

"I'm going south," he replied. "I reckon when the sheriff

finds out what happened, he'll head straight for the ranch. But that'll be sometime in the morning. He won't wait there long. He'll come on after me," His tone was ironical.

Connie's eyes flashed, and she drew a long breath. "I'm going with you, Lennister," she announced.

He eyed her in astonishment. "But it won't do any good, Miss Connie," he protested. "You'd only be taking a chance and be in the way . . . don't you see?"

"You're going to Rattle Butte?" she asked, business-like.

"I reckon that's my first stop," Lennister answered.

"I'm going to the Bar Cross," said Connie in a determined voice. "I'm going to hear what Claude Graham has to say from his own lips, and I'm going to find out if Graham meant it when he sent word to Robbins that he could take the cattle back without being molested. If I can't ride part of the way with you, Lennister, I'll ride all the way alone."

Lennister frowned and argued, but Connie refused to change her mind or to retreat from her purpose.

"All right," said Lennister in a nettled tone at last, "let's go."

They rode steadily southward in the hour before dawn. When they were west of the butte, Lennister called a halt and considered the girl gravely. "I don't like to let you go on down there alone," he said in a puzzled voice, "although I don't reckon Trope's there."

"I can take care of myself," said Connie tartly. "Since you've got your own gun, you might give me Dad's."

Lennister's eyes sparkled with admiration as he handed her the weapon. But the frown of perplexity returned immediately. Then, from the east, came the distant echo of a shot. He stiffened in the saddle. There came another echo—and another. They were shooting at Rattle Butte. Lennister looked at the girl quickly. "That shows where Trope is," he said. "I've got to slope over there. I can't leave you here. I. . . ."

"You'll have to hurry!" cried Connie. "Don't bother about me."

She drove in her spurs and galloped southward. After a moment or two of indecision, Lennister struck due east toward the butte. He rode like the wind, edging a bit to the south to keep the butte and the trees between himself and the Bar Cross men who, he suspected, were on the east side of Rattle. He heard no more shots, and reached the grove of trees under the west wall of the butte safely. There he dismounted and looked up the sheer side of the butte toward the top. A tall cottonwood grew close to the wall. He took his rope from the saddle, threw it over the lowest limb, and quickly pulled himself up into the tree.

When he reached the highest branch that would support his weight, he could see the overhanging bushes some distance above him. He whistled. It seemed out of reason that there would not be a look-out on the west side of the butte, and that the look-out should fail to see him as he rode from the west. He whistled again and again shrilly. He knew it would be next to impossible to reach the top of the butte by the east slope, for it was undoubtedly watched both from below and above. Even if he started up it, the Triangle men would be most liable to mistake him for one of the Bar Cross outfit. These thoughts were forgotten the next instant, however, when he received an answer to his signal.

He called his name loudly. "It's Lennister! Throw down a rope, do you hear me? A rope. Tie it to something up there, so I can climb up."

He caught an answering voice, and after what seemed a wait of hours, the end of a rope came down and dangled just out of reach against the wall. Lennister gathered himself on the weaving branch, swung the top of the tree gently, and then sprang. He caught the rope, slid down a foot or two, got a grip with both hands, and climbed to the top of the butte.

There he found the Triangle cowpuncher who had secured the upper end of the rope to a stunted pine. He commandeered the man's horse and dashed across the tableland through the cattle just as a volley of shots cracked on the still morning air—a sinister welcome to the first gray shafts of daylight.

CHAPTER TWENTY-SEVEN

Lennister found Robbins and most of the Triangle men grouped on either side of the upper end of the slope, where they could sweep the ascent from the shelter of the bushes. Robbins quickly explained that the Bar Cross outfit had twice tried to rush the slope, and had been driven back with at least two wounded and one horse shot down in the fusillade poured from the top of the butte.

"Trope's with 'em," said Robbins excitedly. "They've run the Bar Cross cattle off east toward the badlands of the river. A man who said he came from Graham was here last night and came up with a white handkerchief on a stick. Said Graham said we could move our cattle north without any fear of trouble. Then the Bar Cross crowd began to show up, and I decided to stay pat."

Lennister had taken in the situation while Robbins was speaking. The Bar Cross herd was a blot on the plain in the northeast. Riders could be seen beyond the trees at the lower end of the slope. Trope was playing a trump card in his endeavor to get at the Triangle cattle, but Lennister was at a loss to understand his motive. He could not expect to run off the herd in broad day; it would hardly do him any good to get the Triangle herd on the south range if Graham had ordered otherwise. Trope's action could signify but one thing—a mad desire for revenge.

The sun had come up and the broad plain was like a sea of gold. The hostile riders disappeared in the shelter of the trees, and a perfect stillness settled down. This lasted for a little more than an hour, while Lennister pondered over Trope's latest move and the theft of the $5,000 from Connie Cameron. Trope had been in Ransford the afternoon and evening before, as Lennister had learned from the sheriff. It had been he who had made the complaint to Strang concerning the shooting of Claude Graham. The messenger who had accompanied Dr. French back to the Triangle had doubtless met Trope on the latter's return down the road from town, and had acquainted him with the girl's action in starting for town with the money. Lennister felt certain that Trope had had a hand in the theft. If so, he most likely had the money on him.

During the next hour or more Lennister tried to evolve a plan to get at Trope, but was unsuccessful. Then, suddenly, two riders dashed from the shelter of the trees across the lower end of the slope to the north side of the butte, where the brush shut them off from view.

"Tell the men not to fire at anyone unless they start up the slope," Lennister instructed Robbins.

But this order was not necessary, for the expected assault did not materialize. Instead, a new and more formidable method of attack soon developed. One of the Triangle men cried out and pointed below the northeast corner of the butte. The others looked and saw a thin streamer floating like a veil in the air. A wisp of the veil floated over the butte, and then the Triangle men knew. It was smoke. Hardly had they realized this when another streamer drifted up from the southeast corner of the butte. The smoke grew rapidly in volume, and soon tongues of flame could be seen licking at the buckbrush and grass at the sides of the slope. Then a sheet of fire seemed to rush across the lower end of the slope, from either side, then meet in the center, and come slowly upward as the wind freshened.

"They're going to burn us out!" shouted Robbins.

In a flash Lennister had seen through Trope's design. He would attack under cover of the fire, in the confusion of smoke and flame. The grass was long and dry, and the bushes on the sides of the slope were dry as tinder. Already the fire was racing up each side. The grass was burning fast, and the light wind threw volumes of smoke across the top of the butte.

"Take your coats, saddle blankets, anything, and kill that grass fire when it gets up here!" he yelled. "Don't mind the brush. Kill that grass fire!"

Behind them the cattle were sniffing the air and shaking their heads. Soon they were milling, and one steer dashed past and down the slope through the fire, bellowing madly. In an incredibly short space of time the fire had swept up the slope. The Triangle men fought to put it out with coats and hats and a few saddle blankets hastily gathered. The smoke rolled in upon them, choking them, and the sun was a red ball through the murky screen shot with the fiery tongues of flame.

The pound of hoofs came from below the smoke screen.

"Let 'em have it!" shouted Lennister above the din.

Guns blazed and bullets cut through the screen toward dark forms. Then there were horses—rearing and plunging in the smoke. Men leaped and ran and were singed in getting through the sheet of fire that swept on across the big tableland. Then they sent a volley into the riders who were trying to control their horses. Some went down, others turned back. The raiders returned the fire, and several Triangle men dropped.

Trope's voice could be heard roaring somewhere ahead of the flames, and Lennister ran across the hot ground toward the spot. Smoke and flying embers now swept in from the brush at the upper corners of the slope. The smoke became so dense that it was impossible to distinguish friend from foe, except at close quarters. Then came the thunder of hundreds of hoofs, and a cry went up.

"The cattle!"

Horsemen dashed back down the slope, and Triangle men afoot ran to drag those on the ground out of the path of the herd that was making for the only means of leaving the burning tableland. The fire had reached the pond, had burned faster on the north side, where the trees were sparse, and was driving the maddened steers around to the south of the pond from where they started in a wild stampede for the slope.

Lennister caught a horse that proved to be the one he had ridden across the tableland, and was soon in the saddle. Others of the Triangle outfit ran for the trees, where many of the horses had sought shelter, and in the space of moments half the men were mounted.

As they rode back toward the head of the slope, they were caught between two sections of the stampeding herd. Cattle were plunging down the slope below them, and cattle were thundering down upon them from above. Lennister motioned to the men to ride down the slope. His gun was in his hand, and he was on the alert for one member of the Bar Cross crew—Trope. Where was Trope?

The Triangle riders followed him down. At the lower end of the slope the cattle plunged into the trees, around both sides of the butte, ahead on the plain. Shots came from the right, and Lennister spurred his horse in that direction. He caught a glimpse of two riders coming toward the trees, and recognized Connie Cameron and Frank Graham. The Bar Cross owner was waving his hand and shouting. Then Lennister saw a horseman dart from the shelter of the trees. Graham's shout came to Lennister on the wind.

"Stop it!"

The horseman's hand went up, there was a sharp report, and Graham slumped in the saddle. Lennister recognized the man who had fired the shot. It was Trope—gone mad with rage, his eyes wild, his big gun sweeping in circles over his head as he plunged back into the trees with Lennister after him.

But Trope's action was a ruse, for as soon as Lennister had entered the timber, he rode out once more, and this time he headed north toward the butte. Lennister saw him pass in the open and changed his course, emerging from the trees as a number of horsemen came galloping around the west side of the butte. It needed no second glance to recognize the sheriff's posse. They came full tilt, and Trope doubled back.

Connie Cameron was now directly in his path. She had dismounted and was standing over Graham, who was sitting on the ground. Lennister cut across, and his heart swelled into his throat as he saw the girl bring out her father's gun. He drove in his steel, urging his horse to its last powers of speed in a mighty spurt.

Trope saw him coming, swung his gun over his left arm, and fired. The bullet whistled past Lennister as another shot broke upon the air. Lennister saw a curl of smoke from the gun in the girl's hand, and Trope's horse reared, sending his rider's second shot into the air above. The horse came down upon its knees, throwing Trope over its head. The man got to his feet as Lennister landed near him after a flying leap from the saddle.

"Drop that gun, Trope!" cried Lennister. "You're through!"

Trope's eyes were two points of darting fire, but he slipped his gun into its holster. Lennister could hear the sheriff and his men bearing down upon them. He put up his own weapon to wait.

As he did so, Trope's right hand moved like lightning. A loud report shattered the momentary stillness. Two thin smoke spirals curled upward from the hips of Trope and Lennister. Then Trope's gun dropped and fell from his grasp. He stood for a moment with a surprised expression on his distorted face, and then he sank to the ground.

From behind him, Lennister heard Connie Cameron's low cry. Then the sheriff and his men were about them.

CHAPTER TWENTY-EIGHT

Frank Graham stared at the circle of faces about him with a dazed look. He smiled faintly at Connie Cameron, who held out a drink of water. He drank slowly, with his hand on the emergency bandage about his chest. Then he scowled at Sheriff Strang and spoke unsteadily.

"I . . . sent word . . . to Trope . . . to lay off," he said. "He took matters . . . in . . . his own hands. It made him mad . . . I guess. He wanted his . . . own way. I . . . had Lennister . . . pegged wrong. It's . . . all a big mistake . . . Sheriff. My fault. . . ."

His words died away, and the sheriff told him not to try to talk any more. "We've sent a man to the ranch for a spring wagon, but I guess one of my men can take you on a horse," said Strang. "I can't see that you're hit fatal, Graham, just keep a stiff upper lip."

They got the wounded ranch owner on a horse with one of the deputies and started him for the Bar Cross, accompanied by two other riders, in case they should be needed.

The Triangle men and some of the posse were herding a number of Bar Cross men who had surrendered in the confusion after the loss of their leader. Connie Cameron stood at Lennister's side, her hand upon his arm. Sheriff Strang stared at them with a frown.

"Did you help Lennister break jail?" he asked the girl abruptly.

"I loaned him a gun, Sheriff," replied Connie with a smile.

"Without knowing what he was going to do with it, I suppose," said Strang sarcastically.

"You as much as said I could bail him out," said the girl sweetly.

"But not with a gun," snapped Strang, looking from one to the other.

"Listen, Sheriff, I reckon we three better talk this thing over alone," said Lennister with a glance at the others about them. "It's . . . sort of private."

The sheriff hesitated, then waved the others away.

"Now tell him about the money," said Lennister to Connie as he drew tobacco and papers from his shirt pocket.

Strang listened with widening eyes as the girl explained about the money she had taken from the safe, and how she had been robbed of it.

"With the money gone and the cattle in danger, and the time so short, I had nothing else to do but get Lennister out, Sheriff," she finished. "I'm . . . glad I did it." She held her head high and looked at him defiantly.

"You should have come direct to me," said Strang, without looking at her. "Do you think you can pick that messenger out of the Bar Cross bunch we've got here . . . that is, if he's with the crowd?"

"I'm sure of it," replied the girl.

The trio walked to where the prisoners were being held. Both Connie and Lennister recognized the messenger at the same time.

"Who got the money?" asked the sheriff sternly, without any preliminaries.

The man scowled darkly and remained silent.

"Who got the money?" Strang repeated in a louder voice. Then, when the man refused to talk, he turned to a deputy:

"Search him, then handcuff him, and we'll take him in. There are more counts than one we can hold him on."

"Trope got it!" the man blurted as he caught the glint of the light on the steel in the deputy's hands.

"You rode ahead and met him coming out from town?" asked the sheriff.

The man nodded as the deputy put the handcuffs back in his pocket.

The sheriff motioned to Lennister and the girl to follow him. He left them at a little distance while he examined the person of Trope, lying on the ground where he had fallen. When he returned, he placed the packet of bills in Connie's hands. Then he turned to Lennister.

"About the best thing you can do now is take Miss Cameron home," he said. "But I warn you not to leave the Triangle until you have my permission."

Days passed and summer came to the Blue Dome country. Will Cameron so far recovered his strength that he could sit out on the porch. The Triangle beef herd grazed peacefully on the luscious grass between the river and Rattle Butte. Claude Graham rode up one day, looking a little pale, and brought the news that his father was long since out of danger. He told Connie how he had issued an ultimatum to his father and had threatened to leave the ranch for good if he didn't order Trope to release the cattle and stay on the Bar Cross.

"Your father told me that the morning I rode down there to see him," Connie said to the youth with a smile. "And the sheriff told us how you both had told him all. It was square of you, Claude."

She held out her hand, and he took it gladly.

Will Cameron sent back a written request that Graham join the Teton Stockmen's Association, and explained that the location of the Bar Cross so far south of the Blue Dome range had caused the association to overlook him. Graham sent back a cordial note of acceptance. Then Connie and Lennister visited the Bar Cross, and Graham offered Lennister the place of manager of his ranch.

"I'll think it over," Lennister told him.

They rode back with the sunset flaming over the western peaks.

"Might be a good job," Lennister told the girl.

"Possibly," said Connie, her eyes sparkling. "But you're acting as foreman of the Triangle, you know, and, besides, you can't leave until the sheriff gives you permission to go."

"Shucks, the sheriff's got all over being peeved," said Lennister. "He knows all about everything. He'll tell me I can go anytime, now."

"Will he?" said Connie with a superior air. "You just ask him. I happen to know he won't give his permission."

Lennister looked at her in surprise. "I could go anyway," he reflected. "But what makes you think he'd tell me I couldn't go, Connie?"

"I told him *not* to," said Connie softly, looking straight ahead.

Lennister caught her horse by the bridle and brought it to a stop. Then he looked at her, and it might have been the glow of the sunset that put the roses in her cheeks.

"You want me to stay, Connie?" he asked slowly.

"I want you to stay, Lennister," she responded.

"Gun reputation . . . and all, without knowing any more about me?" he asked wonderingly.

"I know more about you than you think," she answered in a low voice. "I know . . . oh, Lennister. Blue Dome and the Triangle is as good a place for you to stay as any . . . don't you think?"

Lennister's hand touched hers on her knee. "I wonder," he

said in a low voice. Then, as her fingers closed about his: "I reckon I'll stay, Connie."

Their silence spoke in its own way as they rode slowly back to the Triangle.

ABOUT THE AUTHOR

Robert J. Horton was born in Coudersport, Pennsylvania in 1889. As a very young man he traveled extensively in the American West, working for newspapers. For several years he was sports editor for the Great Falls *Tribune* in Great Falls, Montana. He began writing Western fiction for Munsey's *All-Story Weekly* magazine before becoming a regular contributor to Street & Smith's *Western Story Magazine*. By the mid-1920s Horton was one of three authors to whom Street & Smith paid 5¢ a word—the other two being Frederick Faust, perhaps better known as Max Brand, and Robert Ormond Case. Some of Horton's serials for Street & Smith's *Western Story Magazine* were subsequently brought out as books by Chelsea House, Street & Smith's book publishing company. Although all of Horton's stories appeared under his byline in the magazine, for their book editions Chelsea House published them either as by Robert J. Horton or by James Roberts. Sometimes, as was the case with *Rovin' Redden* (Chelsea House, 1925) by James Roberts, a book would consist of three short novels that were editorially joined to form a "novel" and seriously abridged in the process. Other times the stories were magazine serials, also abridged to appear in book form, such as *Unwelcome Settlers* (Chelsea House, 1925) by James Roberts or *The Prairie Shrine* (Chelsea House, 1924) by Robert J. Horton. It may be obvious that Chelsea House, doing a number of books a year by the same author, thought it a prudent marketing strategy to give the author more than one name. Horton's Western stories are concerned most of all with character, and it is the characters that drive the plots rather than the other way around. Attended by his personal physician, he died of bronchial pneumonia in his Manhattan hotel room in 1934 at the relatively early age of forty-four. Several of his novels, after Street & Smith abandoned Chelsea House, were published only in British editions, and Robert J. Horton was not to appear at all in paperback books until quite recently. *At Prairie's End* will be his next **Five Star Western.**